7/10
12/13

DATE DUE

SH 10-11

8 JA 1-13

GAYLORD   #3523PI   Printed in USA

Desert Ice Daddy
DANA MARTON

First published in Great Britain 2010
Large Print edition 2010
Harlequin Mills & Boon Limited,
Eton House, 18-24 Paradise Road,
Richmond, Surrey TW9 1SR

© Dana Marton 2009

ISBN: 978 0 263 21588 5

Harlequin Mills & Boon policy is to use papers that
are natural, renewable and recyclable products and
made from wood grown in sustainable forests. The
logging and manufacturing process conform to the legal
environmental regulations of the country of origin.

Printed and bound in Great Britain
by CPI Antony Rowe, Chippenham, Wiltshire

DANA MARTON

is the author of more than a dozen fast-paced, action-adventure, romantic suspense novels and a winner of the Daphne du Maurier Award of Excellence. She loves writing books of international intrigue, filled with dangerous plots that try her tough-as-nails heroes and the special women they fall in love with. Her books have been published in seven languages in eleven countries around the world. When not writing or reading, she loves to browse antique shops and enjoys working in her sizable flower garden.

To find more information on her books, please visit www.danamarton.com. She would love to hear from her readers and can be reached via email at DanaMarton@DanaMarton.com

This book is dedicated to my
wonderful writer friends:

Rita Herron, Elle James
and Ann Voss Peterson.

Working with you on
Diamonds and Daddies was
an honour (not to mention fun).

My sincerest gratitude goes also
to my editor, Allison Lyons.

Chapter One

A half-dozen men were dead. And some of the clues pointed to a business associate of his, a man he had vouched for. If even the hint of terrorist involvement surfaced, it would end Texas Double A Auctions, the business Akeem Abdul had built from the ground up, the one thing most important to him. Jabar was a friend—which was the most difficult part of the whole damned affair to accept.

The darker side of his nature bubbled close to the surface, but he quelled it as he always had.

"I want a name, Mike." Akeem drove along the deserted Texas country road faster than he should have, sending up a cloud of dust behind him.

"I'm working on it," his head of security responded via the speaker on his cell phone. "I'm checking into who has the most to gain by messing with us."

Akeem stared ahead, barely seeing the road. He'd been turning that question over and over in his head all morning. Having enemies was nothing new in his book. At thirty-one, he was old enough and successful enough to have acquired a few. When his equine auction house grew to be the largest in the state, not everyone celebrated with him. In Texas, horses were serious business, about serious money, whipping up plenty of emotions.

And he was an outsider, which some people seemed determined not to let him forget.

"I want to be contacted the second there's any development," he told Mike, then thanked the man and hung up as he turned onto the tree-lined private road that led to Diamondback Ranch.

A dozen or so exceptionally fine quarter horses grazed on either side of the road. And as he got closer to the heart of the ranch, reaching the first group of paddocks then passing them, his mind began to clear until it was no longer filled with thoughts of betrayal or security concerns. One image scattered all other thoughts without effort: Taylor McKade. They'd ridden fence together not far from here back in the day, her golden hair flowing in the wind. A smile on her lips…

He blinked his eyes to dispel that vision.

Their fence-riding days were over. He would do well to remember that.

He had seen Taylor only a handful of times in the past five years, briefly each time, exchanging only the most polite pleasantries. Their meetings had left him cut off at the knees. Damned if he knew how anyone could stand being next to the only woman he ever loved, knowing she was married to another man.

He shook his head and spoke toward the horses in the distance. "Here we go again."

His standard operating procedure was to stay away every time Taylor came to the ranch, which hadn't been too difficult until now. She didn't visit her brother's place all that often, and Akeem's business here was only occasional. Flint McKade, his best friend, the man who had built the five-hundred-acre Diamondback, did considerable business with Akeem's auction house, but they tended to meet in Houston for that. Especially of late.

But Taylor had left her husband and was now staying at the ranch with her four-year-old son, for good. And the business that had brought Akeem here could not be postponed this time. Which meant they were going to meet again.

Today.

Now.

He drove his white Lincoln Navigator down the gravel road, noting the quiet of the ranch. Two horses danced in the nearest corral, kicking up dust that flew high and wide. The ground was as dry as it ever got, rain desperately needed but not in the immediate forecast. Flint had worried about that last night when they had talked. Not that his friend didn't have his hands full enough with other things just now. Most of the men killed had been his employees.

The straight, empty road didn't require much attention, so Akeem could allow his gaze to roam the rolling land. Not a ranch hand in sight. Nothing unusual about that around lunchtime. But with all the trouble the ranch had seen lately... His muscles tensed again. He couldn't shake the sense of unease that filled the air. His instincts had been honed in the wilds of the Arabian Desert as well as in Houston's corporate arena. Something was off.

He rounded the last building, mentally preparing himself for facing Taylor as the main estate house finally came into view. He bypassed the circular drive in front and drove to the back, to the entry used by family and friends.

Two police cars sat in the drive.

Gravel crunched under the tires as he stepped hard on the brake. He caught himself, eased his feet off the pedal and rolled up next to the police cruiser on the right.

Took his time looking.

He'd talked to Flint last night. They'd agreed not to call in the police yet on the latest clues that had surfaced. They had decided to try to sort things out on their own first, not knowing who their enemies were, resolving not to trust anyone for now, not even the police. Brody Green, the detective assigned to investigate the murders, had been only too quick to assume that Flint had been involved in the sabotage at the ranch as part of an insurance scheme. Flint had since been cleared, but now suspicion stood a chance of falling on Akeem and his company, and he was wary of how fair-minded the good detective would be. And Flint had backed him up on that a hundred percent.

Flint's pickup wasn't even here.

So what were the cops doing at the ranch? The sense of unease he'd picked up driving in grew into full-blown foreboding. Maybe they brought news about the murder investigations. The killer had been caught, had died in the final confrontation, but nobody knew yet who had paid him to accomplish his grisly deeds.

Akeem pushed the door open, the wall of heat hitting him in the face. His designer leather loafers barely made noise as he stepped out of the car.

He inhaled the scent of ycllow roses that bloomed near thc back of the house and caught sight of a silhouette behind the screen door as he headed up the stairs. He would have recognized her a mile away.

His heartbeat sped.

Crazy. He wasn't a penniless, tongue-tied twenty-year-old with a crush on his best friend's little sister anymore. He was a grown man, successful in his own right, morc than able to provide for a family of his own. He drew a slow breath on that thought. One of these days, he was going to seduce Taylor McKade so thoroughly that she'd agree to marry him, and then he was going to spend the rest of his life making her and her son happy.

But not yet. He said the words in his mind so every part of him would be clear on that. First he needed to exonerate his company from any suspected involvement in the sabotage at Flint's ranch. Then he had to get around the fact that she was his best friend's little sister. In the off-limits category. Firmly.

Not that knowing that made him think about her any less.

But he wanted only the very best for her, to make her life easier, not more difficult. So for now, as they had been for the past couple of years, whatever feelings he nursed were his problem. Taylor's life, with the divorce and all, was enough of a mess. He didn't need to add to it.

He expected a polite encounter of "How are you?" and "Fine," the way it went between old friends who had come to feel awkward around each other.

So he was caught off guard when the screen door banged open and Taylor flew barefooted down the stairs. Her eyelashes were wet, her eyelids swollen. His protective instincts rose as quickly as a sandstorm. And just like that, the business troubles that had brought him to the ranch were forgotten.

"Akeem!" She launched herself into his arms like old times and hung on for dear life.

"What is it?" He locked his arms around her in a protective position, barely daring to breathe for fear of scaring her off. His gaze cut back to the cop cars again. *If someone had hurt her, so help him God...*

"We can't find Christopher." Her voice was a sea of pain. "They—" She pressed her full lips together and pulled away to wipe the underside of her eyes with her fingertips. "The police say he might have been taken."

He could tell what it cost her to say the words, to even consider the possibility that her son was in the hands of a kidnapper. Cold anger filled his body until his muscles became rigid. "By whom?" His thoughts went to her ex, one scrawny neck he would be only too happy to have an excuse to wring. If that bastard—

"They don't know." Her huge, cornflower-blue eyes swam in desperation. She'd pulled back a few inches, but stayed in the circle of his arms. She was just as impossibly beautiful as the first time he'd seen her, her mouth just as tempting, her curves just as perfect— or more so. Motherhood had given a subtle change to her shape, a change he loved. Even in the throes of distress, she was a stunning woman. But at the moment, she needed more than his admiration.

He filled his lungs. "What can I do?" She had to know that he would do anything for her.

"I'm sorry." She winced and pulled back a little more as the first thoughts of self-consciousness seemed to appear. "I'm falling apart, aren't I? I can't fall apart. Christopher needs me." She closed her eyes for a moment, but let him keep her hands.

There was a pause, then up came her gaze. She blinked away the moisture that had gathered in the corners of her eyes. "I'm a total mess."

Yes, she was, but she still stole his breath. He did his best not to show how hard he'd been sucker punched by the sight of her, by the feel of her hands in his. "Where is Flint?"

"Out looking. Everyone is, even Lora Leigh and Lucinda. I'm the only one here, with two officers."

That explained the conspicuous lack of ranch hands around the animals. "Kat?" he inquired, referring to the friend Flint had hired as a favor to him. It sure had to be hot out there.

She nodded. "Kat Edwards, too. They're out in the far pastures and combing the brush and the woods at the west corner of the ranch. Flint wouldn't let me come." Frustration stole into her voice.

"The boy might have wandered off. He could be sleeping in a hayloft. He could come waltzing back in," he said as he led her toward the door, getting her out of the merciless noon sun. Hell of a time of the year for anyone to get lost out there, especially a child.

"They already checked the central buildings," she said, but he could see a glint of hope in her eyes. "They started here as soon as I couldn't find him."

"When?"

"Three hours ago." Tears welled but didn't spill to her cheeks, as if suspended by sheer will. The moisture had her eyes shining like a pair of rare blue diamonds.

He opened the door for her and ushered her in. Three hours and Flint hadn't called him. He couldn't help thinking of the damn information that tied the sabotage of Flint's business to his. The thought came as a sharp jab. He shook it off as his gaze fell on his Aggie ring. He might have often felt like an outsider with others, but he never had to feel that way with Flint, with his friends. Flint had his hands full. "What can I do to help?"

She pressed her lips together for a second, desperation clouding her eyes. "Bring him back to me." The small, sour smile borne on pain that twitched up the corner of her lips for a second said she knew she was asking the impossible.

"I will," he promised without thought. Because there wasn't anything on this earth he wouldn't do for Taylor. In this, he didn't know impossible. He was already on the phone, calling Mike back. "I need you over here at Diamondback. Drop everything else. Bring every man you can."

He hung up as he walked down the hall into the state-of-the-art kitchen that was the heart of the ranch.

"And you are?" The graying, slightly overweight police officer at the table set down his radio and looked Akeem over with open suspicion in his squinty eyes.

Being Arab-American, he was pretty much used to that of late, even if he had been born and raised in Texas.

The other cop stopped hooking some machine up to the phone line and checked him out, too. This one was half the other's age and size, with live-wire black eyes.

Akeem focused on the beige plastic unit: a recorder. *Getting ready for the ransom call.*

Taylor didn't miss that, either. She went a shade paler.

"Akeem Abdul. Friend of the family," Akeem said and kept her close.

The first cop's eyes went wide. "The Texas Sheik? No kiddin'." Then he snapped to. "Yes, sir. Officer Peterson."

"Officer Mills." The other one went back to his work after a thorough look that seemed half amused, half disappointed.

Even those who didn't know his face knew the Abdul name from Texas Double A— Akeem Abdul—Auctions. He ignored "Texas

Sheik," the nickname given by his competitors who resented his rapid rise in the ranks and had trouble digesting his Middle Eastern background, that his parents had been Beharrainian.

He pulled a chair for Taylor. The cops were only a minor annoyance. He'd long ago learned to rise above things like that. "Let me get you a drink."

There had to be a hundred men out there already, combing the ranch. He could afford to wait with her until his security force got here and they rode out to meet Flint and join in the search. Christopher would be found. He would see to it.

Why would anyone take the kid? Who? If he could figure that out, they might have a better idea where to look. Which brought him to his next question. "Got a map of this place?"

"Right on the Web site." She sat on a bar stool next to the kitchen counter, her troubled gaze settling on the fridge that was covered with crayon drawings of horses, and got up almost immediately again to pace the floor along the windows that looked toward the back.

She accepted the glass of water he brought her, but didn't drink. The cops minded their own business. Seemed their orders were to stick to the house and wait, which they did with the efficiency of furniture.

Akeem strode to the PC on the kitchen isle—Lucinda, Flint's housekeeper, was addicted to online recipe swaps—and shot straight to the Diamondback home page.

Taylor paused in her pacing. "Flint called you?"

He nodded instead of going into his investigation on murder and the sabotage and bomb parts at Diamondback and how they might be related to his auction house, which he'd come to talk over with Flint. He didn't want to discuss that subject in front of the cops.

He set the form to print fifty copies then pushed the OK button. He wanted to have the maps ready to be handed out when his men arrived.

She was pacing again. Tension grew in the air with every second. He needed something to do. And so did she. "Want to walk through the outbuildings with me?"

She shot him a blank look as if her thoughts were a million miles away. "We already looked there."

Her pain was a tangible presence in the room, like the thick, wet mist of winter mornings that settled into the lungs and made it hard to breathe. He wanted to take her into his arms again, wasn't sure how she would react. Looked like movement was what she needed now to burn off all that nervous energy.

He strode toward her. "We'll look again."

"If there's a call…" Officer Mills frowned.

"Every outbuilding has a phone. If someone calls, she can pick it up from anywhere." He held his hand out to her.

And after a moment of hesitation, Taylor's slim fingers slipped into his palm as if it were the most natural thing in the world, and his hand closed around hers.

He cleared his throat. "Bunkhouses first?"

She nodded and followed him out of the kitchen, slipped barefooted—golden polish on the sexiest toes under the sun, which he should definitely not have noticed at a moment like this—into a pair of worn snake-skin boots by the back door.

Eastern rattlesnake and a black leather top with fancy stitch.

Recognition flashed through him and lodged an odd feeling in the middle of his chest. The boots were spoils of a long-ago riding contest between the two of them.

She didn't look as if she remembered. She didn't look as though she could think of anything but getting her son back. And he would help her. As soon as his security team got here—the best of the best—they would be putting together a plan.

"How did it happen?" Maybe if he kept her talking, she would have less time to worry.

"He wanted to go out to the horses before breakfast." She drew a deep breath as they stepped outside and the heat hit them. "I didn't think much of it when he didn't come back for a while. He's always losing track of time when he's around animals. This place has been like a wonderland to him…" She trailed off as they crossed the yard to the first bunkhouse.

"Christopher, honey?" she called while he systematically searched the place—a manly mess—looking under every blanket, under every bed, in every chest, in every wardrobe.

"Not here. Let's check the next."

She looked up to the sun as they stepped out of the bunkhouse, her face tight. He knew what she was thinking. If her son was out there in this heat, every minute counted.

"And then?" he asked.

"I went looking for him, asking the guys. He'd been out to the colts, but not for long, they said."

"Who saw him last?"

"Nobody's sure. It's busy around here in the mornings. Everyone has a million chores to get done before the heat hits and makes work twice as difficult. Everyone's always rushing around."

They entered the next bunkhouse.

"Christopher?"

He repeated the search, then they went through the same routine again and again with the next building and the next.

His phone rang—Deke Norton, a close friend to the Aggie Four and a trusted business associate. They had a meeting later that afternoon to discuss some mutual investments.

Akeem answered. "Hey, I'm glad you called. I might not make it to our meeting later on."

"Everything okay?"

"Flint's nephew is missing. Probably wandered off."

"Don't worry about the meeting. Let me know if there's anything I can do to help."

"You bet. Thanks, Deke." He ended the call to focus on the task at hand.

"Flint has every man out there looking," Taylor said on her way to the new quarter horse stables that had been built recently to replace the one that'd been burned to the ground.

"The police are helping, too." From the way she said the last sentence, it was clear she was putting her faith in her brother. Smart woman.

"He'll be found."

She had always been nearly as tough as her brother, but as she stopped and turned to him to offer a tremulous smile, she looked fragile and lost all of a sudden. Like she needed him.

His heart flipped over in his chest and he couldn't help getting lost in her cornflower gaze for a moment. She had the clearest blue eyes of any woman he had even known.

He missed them as soon as she turned from him again.

A few horses raised their heads and gave their greeting nicker when she stepped into the barn, clearly recognizing Taylor. Others snorted a warning at Akeem. It had been a while since he'd been out here. Flint brought in new stock all the time. Since the ranch had grown by leaps and bounds, Akeem no longer knew all of the animals.

The smell of hay and feed immediately enveloped them in comfort, but this once he couldn't fully melt into it, and judging by the tight set of Taylor's shoulders, neither could she. Nothing would make her relax until her son was safely back in her arms again.

But she did seem to draw strength from the animals and strode forward with new purpose in her steps, her boots clicking on the stone floor. "Christopher?"

He personally searched every stall. Came up with nothing. "This is going to sound… Have you checked with Christopher's father?" He couldn't bring himself to say the guy's name or even call him her ex.

"First thing." She opened the cabinet doors in the tack room. "And the police went over there, too, to talk to him."

Good. That saved Akeem from having to do it. The thought brought mixed feelings of relief and disappointment.

Her cell phone rang on the way to the new business offices. She picked up the call on the second ring. The way her face went white within the first second, Akeem knew they had trouble.

"Yes," she said.

He stepped closer and put his ear on the other side of the phone, but heard little.

"Is he okay?" The hand that held the phone trembled. "Please don't hurt him. I'll do anything." She listened. "I don't have money. You don't understand."

He could hear shouting then, but not the individual words, caught some reference to Diamondback.

He reached for the phone, but her eyes begged him not to. Slowly, against his better judgment, he let his hand drop.

"Yes." Taylor's voice was a whisper. Tears welled in her eyes, spilled off her dark blond lashes as the phone went dead.

He drew her into his arms because she didn't look as though she was going to make it much longer standing upright. He knew what she was going to say before she ever

Dana Marton 33

opened her mouth, and hot, hard anger rolled through him, aimed at the nameless bastards who would do this to her and would inflict pain and trauma on Christopher.

"They're holding him for ransom," she said.

TAYLOR FELT LIKE SHE WAS underwater, her motions slow, her lungs tight. She felt disoriented. Everything seemed surreal.

Somebody had her baby. Christopher was four years old, proclaiming himself to be a big boy at every turn, but he would be her baby forever. He was the one good thing that had come out of her disastrous marriage. Her love for him was the only thing she was sure of at this point in her life.

And somebody had taken him.

Her tears were not for herself, but for him, for how scared he must be, how he must be wondering where she was and when she would come. Taylor thought, too late now, of asking to talk to her son. The display had shown an unregistered number, not one she could call back.

For the first few moments, she felt only gut-searing pain and despair, then slowly she became aware of the strong, masculine arms around her, the offered comfort that she was too shaken to take. *Akeem.* A long time ago—

She pulled away, unable to think of anything but Christopher.

She was falling apart, wanted nothing more than to curl up in a corner and cry until she was dry of tears, to scream her anger and her fear. But Christopher needed her to keep it together, and she would. She drew a deep, shuddering breath. *Don't think* what if; *don't think what could go wrong.*

She brushed the wetness from her cheeks. "Okay," she said out loud to break the spell of despair that was drowning her. "I can do this. We'll get Christopher back."

"At least we know what happened," Akeem offered.

And he was right. She could put to rest some of the most disturbing thoughts that had been driving her crazy all morning. Christopher hadn't fallen into the river or one of the creeks, he hadn't somehow gotten out to the far pastures and been trampled, he hadn't been bitten by a diamondback rattler or a copperhead.

He was with people who would take care of him because he was their key to the money.

Money she didn't have. *Two million dollars.*

Not that they cared. Her brother had more than enough, and everyone always assumed she had free use of that. Her ex-husband for one. She cut off that train of thought. She didn't have time to waste on Gary. She regretted that she had to call him in the first place, had to listen to him yell his blame at her. He didn't care about either her or their son, but he would use this as an excuse—

Please, God, don't let him get involved.

Forget Gary. At least he wasn't around to muck everything up. A small mercy. She had to focus on how to get Christopher back.

She had never asked Flint for money. It was a point of pride with her. She had asked him for a job when she had finally left Gary, but the accountant position was a job she was qualified for, one she got fair and square. And she was careful to only earn what the previous employee in that position had gotten.

Flint didn't understand her need to make it on her own. Flint hadn't spent five years with Gary Lafferty.

"My divorce was finalized yesterday," she said to no one in particular.

She'd had one perfect day of happiness.

A strange light came into Akeem's dark eyes, but he said nothing.

Flint and he had been best friends since their college days, along with Jackson Champion and Viktor Romanov—the Aggie Four, a tight-knit brotherhood that stood back to back against the world and had achieved a lot more than just financial success. But Viktor was now dead. There was something more there than Flint had told her, and she'd been meaning to ask him again, but had been too busy with settling in, too busy with Christopher.

They had stopped in their tracks, she realized after a moment. She'd been frozen by the voice on the other end of the line. No point in going on with the search now, anyhow. "I should call Flint."

The men should come back in. The heat was brutal, and they had work here. But she couldn't find the energy to dial her phone.

"Want to go back?" Akeem motioned toward the main house with his head. He wasn't as tall as Flint, but was tall compared to her—she was only five-five. He was as lean as a Texas wild cougar and as focused as a striking rattler. And he was on her side, which eased the tension in her chest a little.

"To my office." She moved in that direction. She didn't want to deal with the police. "They said if I say anything to the cops—" She couldn't bear finishing the sentence.

But Akeem nodded even as he pulled out his cell phone. He made a quick call to stop his security force from coming to the ranch, putting them on standby instead.

The cool air in the office building was a relief. She glanced toward her desk, the pile of work she was supposed to handle after breakfast. She liked her work. She liked Flint's ranch. In the three months she'd been here, the place hadn't had the time yet to turn into a true home, but she had found safety among its walls.

Until now.

Christopher.

"Did you recognize the voice?" Again, Akeem pulled out a chair for her, always a gentleman.

"No." She watched him look around and wondered what his fancy corporate headquarters in Houston looked like. Unlikely that she would ever see it. She had no business there. She flipped her phone open. "I need to call Flint."

"Are you sure you don't want to bring the cops in on this?" He seemed to be weighing the issue once again.

"Pretty sure. You didn't hear him. He was—" The voice had been incredibly cold, incredibly hard. The voice of a man who would do anything. Even to an innocent child. Her throat tightened.

"Then you can't call all the men back. The cops will know something happened if the search is called off all of a sudden."

She hadn't thought of that. Her mind was still reeling. Her fingers stopped mid-dial, and she looked up at him, lost in an avalanche of emotions, unable to make a decision in that moment, unable to think beyond her fear.

"We should tell Flint, in any case. Want me to talk to him?"

"Please," she said as he pulled a BlackBerry from his pocket, the latest model. She recognized it only because Flint recently had gotten the same one. Boys and their gadgets. At another time, she might have found it amusing. In this moment, it was barely a blip in her consciousness as her thoughts moved back to her son.

"How would they have your cell-phone number?" he asked.

"It's my work cell. A ton of people have it."

"What else did the man say?" Akeem was dialing already.

"That they would call back."

"Hey, you okay? We got a call here," Akeem

said into the phone. "Don't worry about it. You've been busy. But anyway, I'm here to help." He listened. "Money," he said. "Better stay out there for the cops' sake. Just send a couple of men back. Kat Edwards, too, if you can." Then, "Not yet." And explained the whole situation to Flint.

The invisible fist tightened around her heart again. Some menacing stranger had her son. Her breath stuck in her lungs, and she had to rub her sternum to get air moving again. She had to get beyond this pain so she could do whatever it took to get him back. She had to come up with a plan.

As soon as Akeem hung up with Flint, he was dialing again. "Jack," he told her, then focused on the call when it was picked up. "Does your assistant still have that connection at Nextel?" He paused a beat. "There was a call made to the number I'm going to text message to you in a second. I need to know where it came from. Satellite positioning, whatever. And I need it now. I'm at Diamondback. Christopher was taken." He listened to Jack on the other end. "You bet."

"Can he do that?" she asked, feeling the first ray of hope. She rattled off her cell number and he keyed it in.

"Is there anything Jack can't do?" To his credit, his face showed nothing but confidence.

And he was right. Jackson Champion, shipping tycoon to be reckoned with, a self-made millionaire like Flint and Akeem, wasn't the type to take no for an answer, not ever.

"Where is he?" Jack was always off somewhere, expanding his business.

"Greece. He's in the middle of a deal, but he'll cut the meetings short and come back tomorrow. He wants to be here to help. And he's sending two choppers with pilots from his warehouse in case we need them for anything."

Her throat tightened again. The outpouring of help humbled her, just as it had earlier in the day when close to a hundred of her brother's employees rose as one to drop everything and go find Christopher. She'd been so used to going it alone that the experience left her both grateful and bewildered. That some million-dollar negotiation would be set aside for her was beyond her experience, and yet knowing Akeem's work, he had to be postponing business, too, to be staying here with her. And he was probably the most driven among them.

Gravel crunched as a car pulled up to the main house. Akeem glanced out the window. "Looks like one of the ranch hands came back."

Flint must have sent him. He should return at least a handful of men. The horses would need watering in this heat. Everybody had work to do.

"If you need to be somewhere——" She raised her gaze to Akeem. He looked as solid as a rock fortress: calm, self-assured. He was dressed nicely, leather loafers, black suit pants, white shirt with sleeves rolled just below the elbows——had always dressed nicely, even back in college when he had little money.

He always had an inner, emotional strength she envied, and a handsome, noble face. She had developed a serious crush on him the first time they had met.

"I'm right where I need to be." His voice was quietly reassuring. And his eyes turned a shade darker yet, near black, like she fancied the night sky of the desert might look in the land of his ancestors.

She didn't know what to say. For the past five years, she'd been utterly alone, marriage or no marriage. Akeem had shown her more consideration in the past hour than Gary had in the whole last year they'd been together.

He was a solid presence next to her. And she knew without a doubt that he meant every word he had said. Trusting herself to him, leaning on him throughout this terrible mess, would have been too easy. A few years back, she would have done just that. But Gary had taught her a couple of hard-learned lessons she could not soon forget. Would never forget, she hoped. Because she had sworn she would never let her life get so far out of her own control again.

Shouting drew her attention and she jumped

up to push to the window next to Akeem, aware of his nearness suddenly, but only for a split second. Then cold gathered in her stomach at the sight of the familiar beat-up, green pickup. The man who'd pulled in a few minutes ago wasn't a returning ranch hand.

She recognized the car, as she recognized the voice. And then as he stumbled out of the main house, lurching down the stairs, she recognized that he was drunk once again. The absolute last person they needed here.

One of the cops followed him out of the house to keep an eye on him.

"Who is that?" Akeem was already going for the door, ready to handle the situation to spare her any upset.

Jaw tight, she held him back. "You stay. I'll deal with him."

"I don't think so."

But her hand on his arm did make him pause for a moment.

"It's okay," she told him, although it wasn't. Nothing was all right in her world at the moment. But Akeem needed an explanation, and she needed to deal with the man still spewing obscenities in the yard.

"He is Christopher's father," she said.

Chapter Two

One look at the thunder on Akeem's face told Taylor she better head off conflict while she could. "Would you mind checking on the officers to make sure everything's okay in there?"

"You want me to keep them out of this?"

She watched his handsome face harden as Gary kept calling for her outside. Gary could be difficult to handle when he was like this, and Akeem had never been good at suffering fools. She didn't need a fight on her hands. "Please," she said.

"And you want me to keep myself out of it." Akeem held her gaze, then nodded after another second. "Of course," he said, already walking out the door.

The tension in her shoulders relaxed a little. He wouldn't cause any problems for her. When had he ever not done as she'd asked him? She could only think of one extremely embarrassing occasion, when she'd turned nineteen and gone to a clam bake at a friend's house that morphed into a keg party. She'd come home, wasted, in the middle off the night, snuck into the guest bedroom and practically begged Akeem to take her virginity. He'd been visiting Flint to strategize some deal they were putting together.

Not only had he said *no*—emphatically—

but he ran. He was gone by the time everyone got up in the morning, with some
business-emergency excuse to Flint. They
were wheeling and dealing even back then,
in college.

She always traced the awkwardness that
had entered their easy friendship back to that
night. And she found now that she could still
blush at the memory.

She rubbed her hands over her face before
calling out an "In here" and watching through
the open door as the two men passed and
measured each other up in the yard.

They were nothing alike. Gary was blond,
Akeem darker in coloring. Gary was the taller
of the two but Akeem much better built. Gary
had on a stained, olive-green T-shirt with
equally stained blue jeans. Akeem wore suit
pants with a crisp, white shirt—had probably

come from work. But the main difference was in their faces, in their eyes that reflected the essence of each. Gary's gaze was hazy, anger deepening the lines of his face, his mouth set in a leer, his chest puffed out. Akeem's stance conveyed effortless power, his gaze holding concern for her as he glanced back.

She put on her "I'm fine here" smile. One dark eyebrow slid up his forehead, but then he nodded again as if to say "As you wish" and kept going.

She closed the door behind Gary the second he stepped over the threshold. Just in time.

"Who the hell is that? Your new boyfriend? What is he, Mexican? Ain't there a border patrol looking for him someplace?" He laughed at his own joke, smelling of cigarette smoke and beer.

"One of Flint's friends. Just trying to help." She backed into the room, putting a small table between them that held a handful of flyers for the next open day at the ranch, and two coffee mugs that had been left out. When the alarm had been raised about Christopher being missing, everyone had rushed out to help.

"The pigs in the kitchen say Chris is still missin'. Shouldn't have never let you take 'im. What in hell was more important than watchin' my boy? Playing with your Mexican friend?"

She knew better than to respond to his accusation when he was like this. Her gaze landed on the mugs. "I'm making coffee. Would you like some?"

He took a step forward, none too steady on his feet.

When had he changed from the charming, full-of-life rodeo cowboy to the bitter man he was now, one who regularly got drunk by noon? Once upon a time, he'd been her knight in shining armor, or so she'd thought.

He'd dazzled her with his larger-than-life personality, his outrageous courting and endless promises. Having just inherited money from his father, he'd shown her a side of life she had never known. He'd showered her with gifts and attention when Flint was one hundred percent focused on building a business out of nothing, and Akeem, the man she had a major crush on, always kept himself frustratingly out of reach.

Gary had introduced her to the fast life, and they had been happy for a while. By the time she figured out that they weren't as much in love with each other as they'd thought, Christopher was on his way. Then Gary had run out of his father's money and had no idea how to make more. The drinking began. When Flint had become more and more successful, the demands for her brother's money started. And when after a while she refused, hatred and verbal abuse followed. Then more.

"I miss you, you know," he said with drunk melancholy and walked around the table, put on that rodeo cowboy smile that used to make her heart beat faster, flashed those strong teeth.

She turned to the coffeepot, hoping some caffeine would sober him up.

"If your brother helped us, we could make it together. We should try again, babe." He pressed against her back and put his hands on her waist. "We could make that little girl you wanted."

She slipped out of his hold, away from the stench of stale beer on his breath. "Why don't you sit down? I'll get you a cup."

He followed her to the cupboard, looked around. "We can even live here, if you want to be close to your family. Flint would put up a decent house for you if you asked."

Here we go again. She put the dirty dishes into the sink in the corner and set the two clean cups on the table. If Gary was willing to move to the ranch, that meant he must have run up enough debt to have to worry about losing his house. She felt sorry for him, but she knew now that she couldn't help him. God knew, she had tried. Truth was, nobody could help him until he was ready to help himself, until he was willing to acknowledge his problems.

Gary didn't want help to kick his beer habit. All he wanted was money. Flint's money, to be more specific.

"I know you miss me, babe." He grabbed

her from bchind and crushed her to his chest, dipping his mouth to her neck.

His touch was…irritating. She had trouble remembering a time when it had made her feel anything but disappointed that she had fallen for his seduction in the first place. She'd been young and naïve. Time had cured her of both those problems.

She pushed away, had to put effort into working herself loose. She turned to makc surc he would see in her eyes how serious she was. "We're divorced, Gary. I'm not coming back."

"Why the hell not?" Anger melted the smile off his face. "You screwing someone else?" His voice rose. "That Mexican?"

She tamped down her anger and frustration. She so didn't need this right now.

"I was generous letting you have the boy." His blue eyes flashed. "But you ain't takin' too good care of him. Maybe when they find him, I'll take him home with me."

Her heart clenched, a brand-new wave of fear obliterating all other emotion. She'd been given sole custody, but only because Gary agreed. If he brought it to a fight…

She would smile if it killed her. "Please." She tried to placate him, the role she'd grown into over the years.

And not for the first time, she considered that maybe she should have been fighting all along. Maybe she should be yelling back that he'd given up Christopher only because he didn't feel like taking care of him. He didn't want to be staying home instead of hitting the bars, didn't feel like giving up his beer money to support his son. But she had, from the beginning, always chosen the path of backing down, of accommodation, because giving

Christopher a home with as much peace and normalcy as possible had always been her first priority. So she had compromised, had put on a good face and covered up for Gary as much as she'd been able to.

"Please," she said again. "We agreed. You don't have time to watch him. You're looking for a job. I'll ask Flint to help." Preferably out of state. "Please."

"Please like hell!" he shouted and grabbed the end of the table, sending the two mugs crashing to the floor, tipping the table after them.

The door slammed open the next second, startling her worse than the table had. She had expected *that*. But she hadn't expected Akeem, who stood in the doorway with the sun at his back. His gaze went to Gary first, then to her.

"You need any help in here?" He stepped inside, his shoulders held rigid, his jaw tight.

A whole new level of tension filled the air as she looked between the two.

A dangerous glint was coming into Gary's eyes as he stepped forward. "Yeah. You can help by getting the hell out of my business and staying the hell away from my woman."

She could smell the fighting hormones in the air and couldn't fully trust the men to control themselves. "Just bumped into the table. It was an accident." She stepped between the two.

Akeem said nothing, just straightened the table then squatted for the china shards, placing them in his palm. It appeared that, for her sake, he wasn't going to push the situation, but he wasn't going to leave her alone with Gary again, either.

Which meant that Gary shouldn't stay. She couldn't count on him not to pick a fight, and she couldn't handle that now on top of everything else. But she couldn't in good conscience send him home in his car. He was a jerk, but he was Christopher's father. And even if he weren't, nobody should drive in his condition. Him not caring about his own life was one thing, but there were others on the road.

She glanced toward the main house through the open door where the cops were probably all set up for whatever call might come in. God, she couldn't think about that. She pressed the heel of her palm to her sternum. She wanted to stay here, needed to stay here. She took Gary by the elbow. "I'll get someone to drive you home."

He shrugged her off. "Like hell," he

muttered and was about to say more, but her cell phone's sharp ring cut him off.

Everyone went still, the tension doubling in the room, which was a feat, all considered. Her fingers trembled as she flipped the phone open and lifted it to her ear.

"I want you to bring the cash to Route 109, keep driving until further instruction. We'll be expecting you on Thursday morning, at seven. Come alone or your son dies. Tell anyone and your son dies. Be late and your son dies. Get the picture here?"

Her throat was so tight she could barely say the single word, "Yes."

Today was Monday, was all she could think. She couldn't bear the thought of them having Christopher for three more days. He was just a little kid. Didn't they realize what they were doing to him? Didn't they know that he might never fully recover from this ordeal? And even three days…

"I don't think I can get that much money that fast." She knew for sure, in fact. Flint had money and would give it to her without question—and this once, she wasn't too proud to ask—but he didn't keep his money in cash. She knew—she handled his accounts. He kept some cash for emergencies but nowhere near two million dollars. His money was in horses and land, neither of which could be made liquid in a matter of days.

"You want your kid back, you get the damn money!" The man was shouting now.

Then Akeem was there, taking the phone from her before she realized what he was doing. Alarm snapped through her. This was her son, her business. She didn't trust anyone with this but herself. She grabbed after the phone, missed as he turned. *Oh, God.* They couldn't afford to do anything to upset the man on the other end. She clutched Akeem's arm, scared breathless.

"No, I'm not a cop. I'm your money man. You can have the money today. You tell me where, and I'll bring the ransom," he was saying.

She couldn't hear what the man responded on the other end.

"If you want the money, I'll drive her." Akeem's voice was hard power.

He listened again.

This was so not going to work. Whoever had her son was the one calling the shots. They shouldn't have done anything to make them angry. If this hurt Christopher, she could never forgive—

"That's the deal," Akeem was saying, then after a moment, "Okay. We'll be there."

"What happened?" Her hand shook as she reached for the closed phone. The call was over. And once again she hadn't gotten to ask to speak to her son. She could have cried with frustration and fear.

"The exchange will be tomorrow morning at seven. It's the best he would agree to," Akeem said.

She caught her breath at the sudden ray of hope and felt the anger leak out of her. He had somehow worked it so that her son would be home sooner. Still, every minute stretched like an eternity before her, could bring new dangers to Christopher. But sooner *was* better.

"I'll drive you." Concern for her sat in his eyes. "I'm sorry I couldn't do better. They wouldn't let me go alone. They want you there."

She wouldn't let him go alone, either. Christopher was her son. A minefield couldn't have kept her away from him. But there were other obstacles.

"The money—"

"Don't worry about the money." He dismissed that with a shrug, as if two million dollars was nothing to lose sleep over.

"I'm the father. I'll be driving. He's my son. I'll damn well be there." Gary had apparently figured out what was going on, and for a moment he even managed to look together and almost heroic. Then a sly look came over his face. "How much money?"

Akeem said nothing, wouldn't even look at him.

"Two million," she said because she knew that ignoring him would make him start yelling once again. "We are paying the ransom." The idea of having that much money and handing it over to someone was still bewildering, but she would have handed over the Gross National Product—if she could get her hands on it—to save her son.

She couldn't quite believe that Akeem had that kind of cash lying around and was willing to give it to her, but whether swallowing all her pride and accepting it from him or having to beg, steal and borrow—or sell her internal organs to scientific research— she knew she would have that money come morning.

But she had to deal with Gary first. He was the wild card, unpredictable, with a way of always making things more difficult than they had to be. But she would make sure he didn't mess this up.

"If we go to the police with this, those

people will—" She couldn't bring herself to repeat the threats. She couldn't even think of them. She firmly fixed a picture of a positive outcome in her mind. That would be the only thing she would allow herself to focus on. "So don't say anything to anyone. Okay?"

Gary harrumphed, a sullen expression on his face. He didn't like her taking over like this, as she had known he wouldn't. He very much insisted on wearing the pants in the family, whether competently or not, and making all decisions. But for once, she couldn't afford to humor him.

Akeem stepped to the door and held it open. "Let's get going then. We have plenty to do to get ready. I'll take Gary home."

She was so surprised she could hardly move. Instead, she watched them for a second or two.

"I think I..." What she thought was that allowing the two men to leave together was a really bad idea, but she couldn't say that without getting Gary angry and possibly offending Akeem. She didn't want to offend Akeem. It was such a relief to have him around, and he was being so incredibly nice. So she looked for an excuse to keep them apart.

But Akeem said "I'm here to help" in that mild voice of his that was full of calm strength and had always worked miracles with even the wildest horses.

Worked on her, too, even now. She let go of trying to control every detail of the situation and reluctantly nodded.

For a moment it looked like Gary might object, but one look from Akeem actually had him complying with only a few muttered curses, miracle of miracles.

He only tossed in one objection, and that only when he was halfway across the yard. "I ain't leavin' without my pickup."

"Yes, you are," Akeem said in that voice again. "One of Flint's men will drive it over to your place later."

Gary's face was turning red. But even drunk, he seemed to know enough not to pick a fight with Akeem. Or so she hoped. She didn't breathe easier and believe that he was actually going until he got into Akeem's car and slammed the door shut. And still she didn't fully trust them not to do anything stupid on the way. She knew Gary's temper well.

But she was too worried about Christopher to worry any longer about the men.

The white Navigator was just disappearing behind the paddocks as her phone rang again.

H<small>E HATED LEAVING</small> T<small>AYLOR</small>, but if getting her ex out of her face would help her, then that was what he would do, although he would have been happy not to go within a mile of the man. Akeem drove faster than necessary, eager to be rid of Gary.

"So you gonna pay the money for my boy?" Gary had been watching him the whole trip, asking questions between giving directions.

"Yes."

"And what do you expect from my wife in exchange?" he asked just as Akeem pulled into the driveway of what once had been an elegant country house and was now falling into disrepair.

Anger boiled close to the surface. He held it in check, as he normally held all emotion. Because he needed to prove to himself that he wasn't like his grandfather. Because a wild desert warrior would be no use to Taylor. To win her, he had to become what his friends and business associates thought he already was—a true Texas gentleman. "She's my best friend's sister."

"That all? You sure you're not boinkin' her?" Gary gave a grating laugh.

The gentleman veneer was wearing awfully thin. He'd shown admirable self-restraint during the drive, but now Akeem's arm shot out, his wrist catching the man's neck at his Adam's apple and pressing him against his seat. He was glad that Taylor couldn't see him now.

"Maybe it'd be best if we didn't discuss Taylor." He held on to that razor edge of control. Because he wanted to do so much more to Gary than restrain him for the moment.

Like hell Taylor's divorce had been as amicable as she'd been telling everyone. Like hell they'd just grown apart. The bastard was a drunk and he was a violent drunk at that. And if Akeem allowed himself to think what might have happened to make Taylor pick up Christopher and leave…

But he couldn't think of that, because more than anything he wanted to help Taylor now and he couldn't do that from jail.

So he didn't push harder, and he didn't drag the bastard out of the car to— He drew a deep breath and held his anger in check.

"You'll be at the ranch tomorrow morning at six. You'll be sober." He congratulated himself on how reasonable his voice sounded. "You'll stay at the house, keeping vigil with the cops so Taylor can ride out with the search teams. She'll be frantic. She'll say that she can't sit still at the house anymore. And if you tell anyone about the ransom—"

He paused, took a moment to get a firmer hold on his famous calm. "It'd be better for the both of us if you didn't."

Gary's face was turning a pale purple, his watery blue eyes bulging, his lips forming a barely audible "Yes."

With effort, Akeem relaxed his hand, watched the guy scamper out of the car, then he backed down the driveway without looking at that sorry excuse for a man again.

He was dialing his phone as soon as he was back on the highway, calling the bank, telling them to have his money ready within the hour. The next call went to Mike, his security manager.

"I'm going to need a handgun," he said. He had hunting rifles at home, but for this trip to the desert, he had different needs altogether.

"Yes, sir. I'll have one cleaned, checked

and ready for whenever you stop in." Mike was good that way, didn't ask too many questions, but was always prepared to do whatever needed doing.

"I might not make it into the office for the next couple of days." If there was anything Taylor and Flint needed, he would be there for them for as long as they needed it. He could even sleep out there, which he hadn't done in ages.

"Can you bring the gun over to my place in about two hours? Ammunition, too. And two bulletproof vests. One small," he added after some thought.

"Yes, sir."

Taylor would be going with him. He would have been willing to do anything to avoid that, to keep her from danger, but the kidnapper had been adamant. And it didn't make all that much sense. What did they care, as long as they got the money? They probably figured Taylor would be easier to intimidate. They were wrong about that.

He'd seen the steel in her eyes. And didn't want to think about what had to have happened to that tomboyish but still sweet and innocent girl he had once known to put all that hardness in her. Because if he thought about it, he would have to turn the car right around and go back to Gary. Which wouldn't be the most productive thing at the moment, even if it would be the most satisfying.

"Is there anything I can do to help?" Mike was asking.

"Maybe. We'll talk when you get to my place." He thanked Mike and hung up the phone, his thoughts already on the next morning, on what hc needed to do to protect Taylor and her son.

Route 109 led through a vast area the locals fondly called Hell's Porch. While it wasn't an official desert, its thousands of acres supported nothing but some brush and countless scorpions and snakes, some coyotes, quite a few wild hogs and the occasional cougar. The combination of which provided endless possibilities for anyone entering the area to get into some serious trouble.

But aside from all the wildlife, tomorrow it would also hide an unknown number of kidnappers probably all armed to the teeth and a little boy who was likely scared to death.

Enter the woman he loved.

With nothing but him to stand between them and out-and-out disaster.

"EVERYTHING GOOD?" the voice asked.

Jake Kenner grinned into the phone. "Better than good, boss. We're getting the money today." He ought to get a bonus for that. He sure hated waiting. The longer you sat around, the more chances for someone to figure something out or mess something up.

"What in blister-blazing hell are you talking about?"

"They wanted to bring the money early. It's all set up," he boasted, more than pleased with himself. He'd had his doubts about all this at the beginning, but he had handled it well, yessir, and he was really looking forward to that money. He shifted the chewing tobacco along his gum and spit some juice out, careful with his new boots he'd bought in anticipation of the money coming in.

"And who authorized that?" the voice shouted in rage, instead of praising him.

"I th-thought—" he stammered, growing uncertain now. "Sooner the better, ain't it?" He shoved away the jewelry catalog his girl-friend had been leaving around her apart-ment for him as a hint, angry now that he'd brought it along. It'd be just his luck to have the whole job come to nothing and not get the money after all.

"Wasn't I specific with the timing?" said the voice of dread.

He didn't dare respond to that.

"What do you mean, they?" the voice asked then.

"Some guy's gonna drive her."

"For your sake, I hope this is some sick joke you're making up."

He stayed silent again, looking at the kid,

who was watching him with hurt and betrayal in his large blue eyes, always watching. Jake didn't bother with a mask. The kid would have recognized his voice anyway. And since he'd gone missing the same time as Christopher had, everyone already knew that he was involved. He was confident that when this was over, he could buy himself a new identity and disappear forever with his share of the money. He glanced at the boy again. He was a smart little kid, had a way with the horses, too, as little as he was, which Jake, a trainer, could appreciate.

He shrugged off the prickle of conscience. The kid would be back with his mother soon enough.

The boss growled. "Who in hell is coming with her?"

"Probably her brother," he guessed.

"That bastard is out leading the search in a chopper. Watch out for that."

Jake's stomach clenched. The whole business was beginning to look bad suddenly. "You think she called in the pigs? She's bringing an undercover cop?"

"Not a cop," the voice snapped.

And the man ought to know. He'd assured Jake at the start that he had an inside connection with the cops, that everything would be taken care of. Jake would get his money with very little risk of trouble. Which he counted on. He had plenty of trouble from his creditors already.

"Probably some thug his brother hired to protect her. Do whatever you want with him. He's dispensable. But whatever you do, you can't let her and the boy go. I need time. Two more days. Can you idiots understand that?"

He didn't like the tone of warning. He glanced at the other five guys the boss had recruited for the job. One was checking his gun, the other three were still sleeping. When had he become responsible for all of them?

He said the only thing he could. "Yes, sir."

Chapter Three

Taylor slept in fits, on and off, after a tense day where she had to pretend in front of the cops that nothing had happened, pretend disappointment when the men came back to the ranch to take care of the animals and rest, then pretend hope as they geared up for a night search and left again.

Crying in frustration was the easiest part. She didn't have to pretend that.

At least Akeem and Gary hadn't gotten into

a fight on the way to Gary's place. Neither sported any bruises this morning.

She sipped her coffee at the kitchen table, watching them talking quietly in the living room. They'd shown up at about the same time an hour ago. Gary looked sullen, but sober and willing to cooperate, which was what counted. He even had on clean, if wrinkled, clothes, his hat in hand.

He nodded one more time to whatever Akeem had told him, then left him and moseyed over to the cops. Akeem strode to the window. In a room full of tension, he was a bastion of calm and solid strength, his movements unhurried, his attention focused. He'd left his corporate gear behind for once, wearing blue jeans with a sand-colored Polo shirt and boots, reminding her of their younger days. Even in informal clothes, he looked every inch the prince of the desert that he was—a real prince, if estranged—something few knew about him beyond his circle of friends. He liked to keep his private life private.

His silhouette blocked half the window, but she could see through the other half. The ranch hands were waiting outside, the vehicles lined up, Flint out there with them, dividing up the area that needed to be covered. Lora Leigh, his new wife, was at his side, ready to go to bat for Christopher.

Lucinda, the housekeeper, stood out there, too, but only to see everyone off. She'd had a hard time the day before in the heat. She was going to stay home to rest. Only because she knew the score. Beside Taylor, Akeem, Flint and Gary, Lucinda was the only one Taylor had told about the ransom call.

Lucinda was like family. She loved Christopher like a grandmother.

She could think about little else now. In a few hours, she would have Christopher back. She wouldn't allow herself to let any doubt enter her mind. When those thoughts pushed their dark despair into her heart anyway, she closed her eyes and said another prayer, for the thousandth time since Christopher hadn't come back for his pancakes and grits.

"Looks like they're about ready." Akeem stepped away from the window and came over to her.

Gary was leaving his conversation with the officers and wasn't far behind. "Here. Some coffee to take with you." He produced a tartan-patterned Thermos from somewhere. And she recognized it after a moment—a gift from a neighbor a few years back, along with a picnic basket they'd never used.

"Good luck. Be careful." His blue eyes were clear for once, the encouragement in them genuine. He could be nice when he wanted to be.

"Thanks," she responded with a tired smile and accepted the Thermos, although Lucinda had already set everyone up with food and drinks. She ran the house like a general. Thank God for her. She had taken good care of Flint all these years, and Taylor was grateful for that.

She walked to the door behind Akeem, her knees nearly locking, and glanced back before stepping through the door he was holding open for her. She looked to Gary one last time, hoping he would hold up long enough without a drink. "You can call on my cell if anything happens here."

Then she walked out into the morning sunshine and found Flint's gaze on her face, his expression tight with worry. He'd gone a few rounds on the phone last night with Akeem about who should be driving her to the exchange. Akeem had won, but only because he had more experience with Hell's Porch.

Flint hadn't been happy about using someone else's money either, even if it was from one of his best friends, but with the time limit, he had no choice but to accept.

"Sure you don't want me to go with you instead?" Flint being Flint, he couldn't resist asking one last time, adjusting his Stetson on his head.

"I'll be fine with Akeem. Thanks." She headed for the Navigator, said nothing at the surprise that waited for her in the interior until the doors were closed behind them. "What's all this?"

Plasticky-looking, black foot-by-foot squares covered the sides, save the windows.

"Kevlar." He started the engine, but didn't pull out ahead of the pack. They were to lag behind, then take their turn toward Route 109 when nobody was looking.

Her fingertips were numb from nerves.

"You bulletproofed the car?" She shouldn't have been surprised. Akeem had always been a man who paid close attention to detail. The kind of man a woman could come to trust and depend on. Some other woman. After the mess her marriage had turned into, it would be a long time before she completely trusted another man.

"Mike and the boys worked on it last night." He waited until most of the pickups were rolling down the road, raising a cloud of dust, giving the look of a herd of migrating elephants over the African savannah, then pulled to the end of the line. "Flint told me about Jake Kenner."

The name had the power to squeeze her heart. "He hadn't come back in last night."

"And you don't think he got lost."

"Nobody saw him go out, nobody saw him during the search." Flint had called to tell her that just as Akeem had left with Gary the day before. "He hasn't been answering his cell phone. What if he went off earlier? Before the search began?"

"With Christopher?"

She nodded, sick to her stomach from the thought. "Christopher would go with him. Jake is a trainer. He'd been giving Christopher riding lessons." That thought alone made her break out in a cold sweat.

"Flint said he was new to the ranch."

"He came a month before I did." She clenched her teeth, guilt nearly killing her. What kind of mother was she to trust her son to a kidnapper? She should have known, should have paid more attention. Jake had been aloof, but she'd thought only because he was still new and hadn't adjusted to the rhythm of the ranch yet. He'd been patient with Christopher, doing whatever the little boy's fancy was, whatever made him happy.

Every time she gave her trust, someone took advantage, it seemed. But not anymore. "I wonder if he was only kind to Christopher to lure him in."

"It's not your fault." Akeem's voice was steady and sure. "We can't afford to waste energy on blame. What comes next will need one hundred percent from the both of us."

He was right. She drew a deep breath. "You have the money?" She hadn't been able to ask that inside with the cops listening.

They'd been grousing about having to call in the FBI if and when a ransom call did come in. Kidnapping was a federal offense. She'd been sweating bullets, worrying that they might have figured something was up.

"It's in the back," he said.

Of course. She breathed a little more easily, squelching her thoughts of unreasonable desperation that had come to her during the sleepless night. *What if Akeem didn't come? What if he couldn't get all that money? What if he changed his mind about the money? What if? What if? What if?*

But he was here.

She glanced toward the back, could only see the horse blanket that covered whatever was back there. She caught sight of a first-aid kit. For Christopher? She tried not to worry and just be grateful that Akeem had thought to bring it. She should have thought of something like that. But she hadn't been able to think of anything beyond seeing Christopher today, the moment when she could wrap her arms around him.

She was shaky with nerves. Which was no good at all. They'd managed to get away from the house without arousing the cops' suspicion, but the most difficult and dangerous part of their mission was still to come: handing over two million dollars to armed criminals and hoping, just hoping to God, that they kept their word.

"You have that kind of money lying around, doing nothing, you need a better accountant," she said to make herself think about something else.

"Just had it freed up to buy some horses."

She was so preoccupied still, that a few moments passed before his words registered. "Two million dollars' worth?"

She knew he was doing well, but hadn't realized just how well. It shouldn't have surprised her. He was incredibly intelligent and as hardworking as any man she'd ever known. According to Flint, he could have accepted his grandfather's millions and gone to Beharrain to live the lavish life of a true sheik. Instead, he had put his wide shoulders to the work and set his mind to building his own empire. Which he had.

"And worth every penny," he was saying, that goofy look she knew so well coming over his face. Her brother did the same thing when talking about particularly fine animals.

"Who has horses like that?"

"A prince in Saudi Arabia. There's an auction going on."

Guilt assailed again, albeit from another direction. "And you're missing it."

He shrugged.

Of course, missing the auction was beside the point, since he was giving her the money he was supposed to use to bid, she realized. "I'll pay you back." She couldn't even start to worry about how she was going to do that, but she would if it took her the rest of her life.

"It's not necessary." His gaze found hers, held it. "But since I know you're not going to take no for an answer, I'll just say, I have no doubt."

"Good. Because I'm going to make it. I'm working on it."

"We'll all be coming to you begging to borrow, one day."

If she weren't so tense, she would have

smiled at that. The Aggie Four—three now—didn't go around begging. But she was putting herself through college on an academic scholarship, plus putting away every cent she could save, investing based on her newfound knowledge from her studies in finance and on recommendations from her brother. She was going to build an accounting firm that would be the pride of Texas.

Men weren't the only ones with ambitions and the will to make them come true. She was never going to be poor again, and she was *never* going to be at the mercy of another man. Not even her own brother whom she dearly loved and who would have given her anything she asked.

But she wanted to be her own person at last.

Christopher would start school soon. He wasn't going to be teased for Salvation Army clothes the way she'd been. He wasn't going to be picked on because he couldn't afford to take lunch. Someday he would go to college, a good one. And she wouldn't take Flint's money, not for that, not for anything else if she could help it. And she *would* pay Akeem back.

He was falling back as more and more pickups in front of them took various country roads to get to areas they were supposed to be searching today. Then he took the Route 109 turnoff, and they were on their way to Christopher.

Anticipation held her in a grip so tight she could hardly breathe. She startled when the phone rang. Akeem's.

He flipped it open, listened. "Anything

else?" Then, "Do me a favor, give Flint a call and let him know."

"Christopher?" she asked breathlessly when he hung up. Did this have to do with her son? What should Flint be told?

"Jack," he said. "They traced yesterday's call to the same airport where Flint's transport got blown up."

She stared with incomprehension. "Do you think there's a connection?" What did the horses have to do with Christopher?

"Or coincidence. It's the closest small airstrip that takes private business. Security is not nearly as stringent there as in Houston or Dallas."

A new worry hit her then. "You think they flew Christopher out of the area?" Her heart about stopped on that thought.

"Hey." He took her hand for a second,

squeezed it. "They wouldn't take him anywhere. They need him if they want their
money."

True. She made a point to fill her lungs and
relax. And meant to squeeze his hand back
but he'd pulled away by then. Within a few
minutes, she could see the Shell station in
the distance.

Her phone rang.

"Stop at the station. Go to the bathroom.
There'll be a cell phone waiting for you there.
As soon as I hang up, you'll throw your own
phone and your friend's out the window." The
line went dead.

Now that she knew about Jake Kenner,
she'd been listening for his voice, but it
hadn't been him on the other end. This guy
was older, possibly a heavy smoker, judging
by the rasp. Which meant that this all hadn't

been just one desperate guy's bid for quick riches. She told Akeem as much.

"What did he want?" He kept his eyes on the road.

"They want our phones." She rolled down her window and tossed hers out. "Yours, too. They left one for us at the station up ahead."

His lips flattened in annoyance, but he did as she asked, tossing his expensive Black-Berry that she was sure held a ton of important business information.

She winced. "Sorry."

"You have to stop that." He glanced over. "Nothing matters a millionth as much as you and Christopher."

Her heart gave a quick staccato beat, and a sudden sense of warmth melted a spot off the block of ice that had been growing in her chest all morning. She wasn't sure how to respond to Akccm, so she went with changing the subject. "You think they're watching us?"

He turned his attention back to the road. "They could have a man at the station with binoculars."

That didn't make her feel all that comfortable, considering that she had to get out at the station.

They were pulling up to it within a few minutes, nothing but a few square yards of tar top, a square building and six pumps in the middle of nowhere, decorated with a jumble of signs, some of which advertised businesses decades gone.

The place didn't exactly inspire confidence.

"Want me to do it?" Akeem asked.

"They'd look at you funny if you asked for the key to the ladies' room." She drew a deep breath and opened the door, stepped out and tried to look like she wasn't about to fall apart from nerves.

The station looked deserted save for the man behind the counter inside. When she asked, he handed her the key and the large wooden fob it was tied to. "Here you go, ma'am."

She walked out, glanced at Akeem in the car as she made her way to the bathroom on the side of the flat-roofed building. As she put the key in the lock, the thought that there might be someone in there waiting for her crossed her mind. But the door revealed nothing but a single stall and a black cell phone on the sink. She shoved it into her back pocket, nodded to Akeem as she came out, locked the door behind her and hurried to return the key. She wanted to be back in the car by the time they called her again.

They didn't wait long. Akeem barely pulled back onto the road when the phone rang.

"Go to the next intersection then turn left," was all the voice said this time before disconnecting.

AKEEM WATCHED THE road and stretched his fingers to relax them on the steering wheel. A full hour had passed since the kidnappers had last checked in. The road he drove was no longer paved, the soil dry and full of rocks, the SUV's tires kicking up enough dust to be seen from a distance. Most of the vegetation—sagebrush and the like—came only about waist high out there. He could see for miles, which meant he could also be seen. The few clumps of prickly pear here and there shielded little. They were, however, coming up to a small stand of acacia trees, the road cutting right through them, their only chance of privacy if they were being watched.

They hadn't been followed; they were the only car on the road. But there could be people lying low in the bushes. It all depended on how many men were involved in the kidnapping. Two million dollars could buy a lot of help.

He hesitated, not sure whether to say what he was about to say. Didn't want to scare her, but wanted her to be prepared. "If there's any kind of shooting, duck where you're covered with Kevlar. And in case you need to get out, there's a vest for you in the back under the blanket. You should put that on."

He pulled into the trees and stopped the car. "Now." He reached for his own vest. There was no way he could have taken them into the house this morning without the cops noticing.

The vests were thin and flexible, made of the latest state-of-the-art material, unlike the rigid panels Mike had used for the car. He'd prepared by picking a larger shirt that would accommodate the vest, had tried it all on last night to make sure it wasn't too obvious. He tried not to look at Taylor as he stripped, knowing she was doing the same next to him.

He couldn't help if he had great peripheral vision.

The pale yellow bra begged for more attention. He turned the other way.

"Okay," she said after an endless minute.

And without looking at her, he stepped on the gas.

The winding path snaked across Hell's Porch, doubling back now and then, going in loops from time to time, probably cut by four-wheelers that were popular in the area. Ten o'clock rolled around, the heat outside oppressive enough to necessitate air-conditioning in the car by the time the phone rang again.

Taylor seemed to be whispering a short prayer before picking up. She listened then tucked the phone into her jean pocket.

"Stop the car and get out. You're going to walk the rest of the way. Bring the money. If I see a single cop or a single weapon, the boy is dead." She was about vibrating with nerves. "That's all he said."

"Breathe."

She nodded and drew her lungs full of air. "I'm so nervous, my ears are ringing."

"You'll be fine. It's almost over." He pulled off the road, got out and strode to the back, silently cursing this latest demand. He grabbed the two briefcases that held the money. They weren't going to be able to take anything else.

She was standing in front of the car by the time he walked back up there. He stopped in front of her, saw the desperation in her eyes and put the briefcases down to pull her to him, his intention of providing a distant sort of friendly assistance be damned.

She came willingly into his arms.

"Hey," he said into her hair that smelled like green apple shampoo. "Almost there."

He held her as long as she let him—a few seconds, tops; she was too nervous to stand still—then they walked down the dusty road together. Must have walked a full mile, each lost in their own thoughts, before they came to an area where boulders dotted the landscape, decreasing visibility, providing a good hiding place for anyone who was waiting for them. He scanned each rock and wasn't surprised when a red pickup rolled out into the open from behind one of them.

The car stopped, facing them. Two men, wearing masks, sat up front. He didn't see Christopher.

The man next to the driver got out and aimed his gun at Akeem. "Put the money down."

He gave the briefcase that was in his right hand to Taylor instead. He wanted to keep his gun hand free. Despite their demands to come unarmed, he hadn't thought walking into a situation like this without a single weapon would be a good idea.

"Let us see the boy first," he called back.

After a stare-off that lasted a full minute, the man finally nodded and called over his shoulder, "Show him the brat."

Another minute passed before a rail-thin

man stepped forward from behind a boulder on the other side of the road, holding Christopher by the shoulders in front of him.

"Mom?" Christopher's face was smudged with dirt.

"Don't worry, honey. I'm here," Taylor said, then whispered, "That's Jake," to Akeem, moving that way already.

"Not yet. Stay there."

She glanced back at him, confusion and anxiety on her face, but stopped.

"You—" The first guy indicated Akeem with his gun. "Stay where you are." Then he indicated Taylor. "You bring the money to me and you can have the kid."

Akeem hesitated, hating the whole setup. Another man appeared from behind another boulder, gun drawn and pointed at him. And he figured they must have more, at least one more, their ace in the hole.

The men were looking at each other, eyes darting in silent communication. Akeem watched them carefully, not liking the mood in the air. Something was up, but he couldn't put his finger on what. And he had little leverage to bargain for time or anything else, as he was overwhelmingly outgunned, with Taylor and Christopher now smack in the middle of the crossfire should anything happen.

He needed a moment to assess and think, try to figure out what the men were playing for. But Taylor didn't seem willing to wait any longer. She stepped back and grabbed the second briefcase from him before he could say anything, and was already moving forward again.

"Go slowly," he called after her, keeping his voice low enough so the men wouldn't hear what he said. "If anything goes wrong, just hit the ground. Use the briefcases for cover." Then, because she looked like she needed to hear it, he added, "In a few minutes, you'll have Christopher."

But, in fact, that was not what happened.

The rumble of choppers drifted in from the distance, freezing everyone to their spots as they scanned the sky. The sound intensified, came nearer, and within a minute two police helicopters were swooping in, filling the air with dust when they dipped low.

And all hell broke loose on the ground.

Chapter Four

Akeem dived for Taylor, brought her to the ground, propped the metal-sided suitcases in front of them as bullets filled the air. Then had to get right on top of her to keep her there, since she was determined to get away from him and go for Christopher through all the hellish chaos.

Since some of the kidnappers had rifles and opened fire on the choppers, the cops had no choice but to shoot back.

"Stay down!" He had to shout to be heard

over the choppers and the gunfire. "He's going to need you alive."

But instincts overtook common sense and any logic he could have used on her. She clawed at him. "Let me go!" Wild dogs couldn't have kept her from her son.

But he had to, in order to keep her alive. Her lithe body writhed under him, but she wasn't looking at him; her eyes were on her boy. Keeping her restrained took both hands, so he couldn't go for his weapon. Which might have saved them. The kidnappers were focused on firing at the choppers and paid scant attention to the two of them, neither of whom they considered an immediate danger.

"They aren't going to hurt the boy as long as we have the money. We need to get out of here," he said directly in her ear. "Taylor, look at me."

She did, but only to shoot him a look of fury. "Let. Me. Go!"

He couldn't, not even knowing how much she hated him for it at the moment.

"I can get him!" She fought him any way she could, aiming a kick that could have disabled him if he hadn't rolled out of the way, pulling her along.

"Too dangerous," he said, knowing that in this moment there was probably little he could say to talk sense into her.

"I don't care. You don't understand."

"I understand." He got her hands under control with effort.

"Let me go. He's my son." Desperation distorted her face. "I'm not you. You left your family behind. I won't do that."

That last barb hit home and hit deep, but he hung on to her tighter, even as she kicked him in the shin.

The dust and tears mixed to become mud on her face. When he thought she was tiring from her struggle at last, he let go with one hand, crawled backward, pulling one of the briefcases after him, holding it up for cover, dragging her with his other hand. She had enough presence of mind to grab the other briefcase. He half expected her to clobber him over the head with it, but she held it up to give them more cover.

Getting back to the car was out of the question—too far. He scampered toward the nearest boulder that was large enough to block bullets.

An eternity passed before they made it there.

He pressed her into an indentation in the rock and blocked her body with his. The choppers were coming lower, stirring up dust, destroying visibility on the ground. He couldn't guarantee that they would be recognized from above and not be shot at.

He kept his gun silent for the same reason. The cops might shoot back at anyone who fired. Plus, in all the dust, he couldn't be sure he wouldn't hit Christopher instead of the bad guys.

Taylor struggled against his back, probably for a glimpse of her son. He eased forward a few inches so she could see for herself that there wasn't much to be seen. But the small movement did give him a view through a gap between two boulders. One of the pickups was driving away. One of the choppers followed.

Then another pickup pulled away from behind a boulder and tore down the road, in the direction he and Taylor had come from. And another, going a different way. All in all, five identical pickups raced from their hidden positions in different directions, and the two police choppers were not enough to cover them.

By the time they were left alone in the settling dust, he was beginning to understand the kidnappers' plan. He moved forward carefully, gun in hand, Taylor rushing from behind him, trying to read the spent shells on the ground and the tire tracks. He took his time searching through the area, but couldn't tell which pickup had taken Christopher. The boot prints in the dust were a mess. Jake Kenner had probably picked up the boy and tossed him in his car, anyway. There wouldn't be clean prints of a boy and a man, leading to tire tracks.

"He's gone." Taylor stood on the spot where they had last seen the boy, her eyes dark with pain, her voice hollow.

The events of the past few minutes stood like a minefield between them. She wouldn't look at him, just kept searching the jumble of prints on the ground. Minutes passed before she straightened and turned her attention to him. "How did the police know that we were here?"

He hated the accusation in her voice. "Not from me." But he recalled Gary talking to the cops for a while that morning. Could be he didn't like the idea of Taylor going to their son's rescue with another man.

"Did either of the cops touch you in any way, a pat on the shoulder, whatever? Give you anything?"

She shook her head and wiped her forehead. The place certainly lived up to its name. The giant white-gray boulders did a great job radiating the heat of the sun.

He played the morning back in his mind. "Gary?"

She shook her head again, but then after a moment said, "He gave me a Thermos of coffee. It's in the car." They'd been way too wired on the drive over to have more caffeine. "Do you think he would—" She couldn't finish the sentence, the pain of betrayal thickening her voice.

Same as she'd used on him just minutes ago.

Which stung, because, by God, he had never betrayed her. "You can trust me."

He waited for some acknowledgment, anything. A nod.

She was looking at the ground again.

He let another couple of seconds pass before he grabbed up the briefcases. The dust the choppers had blown around tasted bitter in his mouth as it grated between his teeth.

"Let's get back. There's nothing more we can do here."

He carried both briefcases, slowed his gait to hers. On the way here, he could barely keep up. But now she walked as if all life had been sucked out of her. He hated that he'd been here and hadn't been able to do anything. To have her son within arm's reach then lose him again was obviously killing her.

Emotions swirled in his gut, rage against Jake Kenner and the rest of his cronies. Rage that had no outlet, because they weren't here. His heart broke for Christopher. The kid had to be scared to death. And Akeem was scared for him, to be honest. Added to that was another emotion, for Taylor. But Taylor wouldn't let him comfort her. She was shutting him out.

He stole a look at her face, and it was etched in misery.

"As long as we still have the money, they won't hurt him," he said. Unless they'd gotten spooked by the cops and decided to call off the whole operation, cut their losses before they were caught. He wouldn't tell her that, but it was something he had to prepare for.

The walk to the Navigator seemed twice as long. And gained them little. He took in the shot-up tires, every single one of them, and recalled the pickup that had taken off this way. They wouldn't be going anywhere for a while.

"Let's get inside. The air conditioner will still be working."

"Are we stuck here?" She broke out of her numb state only long enough to ask that. She slid into her seat while he tossed the briefcases in the back.

"The cops know where we are. They'll come and get us when we don't show up back at the ranch. They'll come to investigate the scene of the shootout, anyway. There are cars on their way, I'm sure. The choppers just got here ahead of them."

He reached for the Thermos first thing after he walked around from the back and got in, and now he emptied the contents to the ground before closing the car door, starting the engine and turning on the air conditioner. Then he took the damn Thermos apart. Was it possible they'd been bugged and tracked?

"Why would Gary talk? I told him what would happen if he…" She bit back the rest, fingering the Thermos's top, her eyes red-rimmed.

"Could be the cops went around to his place again after I left him yesterday. Maybe they had more questions and he cracked under pressure. Or maybe he didn't trust me with you and Christopher."

He took the silver insert out, but found nothing between that and the outer shell, nothing in the cap. He put the cap back on and tossed the whole thing to the floor in the back. The transmitter didn't really matter at this stage. The damage was done.

"He didn't trust me," she said. "He wanted to be here. I should have—" She shook her head.

The half-finished sentence had him clenching his jaw. She should have what? Come with Gary? Because that drunk idiot would have been better than Akeem? Because he was her ex and the boy's father? Because Akeem had no business being here with her?

And what if she was right? That thought

had him clenching his teeth harder. Because he *had* failed. They didn't have Christopher.

"Whatever happened, happened. We are going to focus on what we need to do to have the best outcome of what happens next."

Inshallah, his uncles would have said. Accept Allah's will in everything; they had told him that countless times during those four years he had spent with his grandfather in the Arabian Desert after his mother's death. *Trust in Allah and keep your camels watered.* In other words, don't worry about things you have no power to change, but be prepared.

"I'll call Flint." She pulled the cell phone from her back pocket, pushed some buttons, furrowed her brow. "I can't make a call." Frustration crackled in her voice. "I think it's fixed so that they can call me, but I can't call anyone." Then the anger seemed to drain out of her as she went pale the next moment. "Do you think he got hurt?"

There had been some blood in the dirt, which she might or might not have seen. Akeem sure as anything wasn't going to bring it up.

"No way." He reached for her hand, but she pulled away almost immediately. The car was filled with the tension between them.

"The cops wouldn't shoot anywhere near him," he said to set her at ease. "And the kidnappers were aiming up, at the choppers. No way any of them could have hit him by accident."

A few moments passed while she stared blankly through the windshield. Then her chest rose with the deep breath she drew. Her eyes hardened as she pulled herself straighter in her seat and turned to him at last. "We are going to get him back."

"Yes, we are."

A long moment passed with silent communication, acknowledging what had happened as well as the need to move past it for Christopher's sake.

"I hate just sitting here," she said.

Which didn't turn out to be a long-term problem. The cell phone in her back pocket rang the next second.

"SAY GOODBYE TO YOUR SON," the voice on the other end was shouting.

"Please don't do this." Instantly, adrenaline was racing through her veins, clenching her whole body together. Fear clasped her heart, blood drumming in her ears. "Please." She swallowed her tears and struggled for control.

She needed to remain coherent. "I didn't talk to the cops, I swear. Please. I don't know how they found us. I'm still here. I still have the money." That was what they needed. She had to keep reminding them of that.

"You made a big mistake," the voice sneered, still hard with anger. "It's over."

The world disappeared from around her for a second, her vision fading to black before coming back again. Christopher was her life. She couldn't lose Christopher.

"Please," she begged, crying now. "I have the money. You'll get everything you want."

A long silence followed on the other end of the line. She held her breath, unsure if the man was still there or if he'd tossed the phone without bothering to click it off.

But then words came that allowed her lungs to fill with air again. "I'll call you back tomorrow. If you go within a mile of another cop, your little bastard will be dead."

"Is he hurt? How is he? Let me talk to him," she pleaded but he did click off this time. The line was dead.

She let her head drop onto the dashboard and struggled with her tears and for control for long minutes before she could collect herself enough to tell Akeem what had happened.

"We better get out of here." He was opening his door already.

"How?" There was no way they could fix the car.

"On foot. You can bet that sooner or later the cops will show up. And when they do, they'll have plenty of questions for us. If the kidnappers are monitoring us somehow…" He looked around and scanned the horizon. "It'd be better for now if we kept our distance from the police." He slid to the ground. "We don't want the kidnappers to see us anywhere near the cops."

"Where are we going?" She followed him to the back where he was unloading some serious gear: two large duffel bags.

He grabbed the first-aid kit from the backseat and shoved it into one of them. "Back to the boulders."

"Are we going to spend the night out here? What's in those bags?" she asked.

"Supplies I usually carry when I ride out to camp. I put them in this morning—I didn't even know why I was putting them in at the time." He shook his head.

Camping. He did that now and then, rode out to Hell's Porch for days at a time. Flint had told her that. She wondered if he missed the times he'd spent with his grandfather in the desert, although he'd always been tight-lipped about those years. He'd never forgiven his grandfather for the way the old sheik had treated his mother.

"So, how well do you know this place?"

"I know some of it." He swung the bags over his shoulders. "It's too vast to be thoroughly known by any one man."

She could certainly believe that. "Won't the police come to the boulders, too?" she asked after a moment, surprised that they weren't there already. Probably still following the pickups.

"Probably, but I want to take another look at the tracks. We need to be going in some direction, might as well follow one of the tracks and at least have a chance of ending up somewhere close to Christopher."

That made sense. She could almost forgive

him for keeping her from Christopher back there. Almost. "I'll carry something, too," she offered.

"The money."

He handed her the briefcases, and she grabbed them, ignoring when their fingers brushed together.

She couldn't think of anything else on the way back to the boulders but of the shootout, of Christopher, of how close they'd been and how scared he must be. She didn't cry. Energy expended on crying would be much better used for fighting for her son when they reached him again.

"He probably wasn't in the first pickup," Akeem said once they reached the boulders and he'd dropped the bags. He was walking around in a wide circle. "They knew a chopper would take off after that."

"And I doubt he was in the last," she said. "They knew we would be staying here, waiting."

"The first truck went this way." He pointed. "The last pickup drove that way."

"And the one that went the way we came passed right by us. It didn't have Christopher."

"Right." Akeem nodded. "And it wasn't driven by Jake Kenner. I have a feeling he would stick with the boy since Christopher knows him. He'd have the easiest time getting Christopher to do what they wanted."

She bit her lips at that. "So that leaves us with two sets of tracks." After the fight she'd been looking for nothing else but a chance to find Christopher's shoe prints in the dust. Now she registered the shells and the bullet holes drilled into the boulders all around them.

And the blood. But not where Christopher had stood. She gave God thanks for that.

She nudged a spent shell with the tip of her shoe as the realization came, and she took her time digesting it, accepting it. Akeem hadn't been holding her back from Christopher. He'd been saving her life.

"We have a fifty-fifty chance. Either this way, or that." He circled back and hooked his bags over his shoulders again. "You choose. But we better get going before the cops get here."

HER ARMS WERE BREAKING, but Taylor wouldn't have let go of the briefcases for anything. They meant Christopher's life.

Akeem carried the duffel bags without complaint, dragging a large sagebrush behind them to cover their tracks. If the cops found them, they could mess up the exchange once again. She didn't think she would get another chance from the kidnappers.

As if by unspoken agreement, they talked about things unrelated to the current situation. Not that she could shut her mind off from obsessing over every second of the failed exchange, or over what would happen when the next call came in.

"So you like it at Diamondback?" Akeem asked. "Settling in?"

"I don't want to get too settled in. I want to get my own place eventually, but I'm loving it."

"Flint loves having you there."

"Flint wants to wrap me up in cotton and keep me in a velvet box." She gave a wry smile. She couldn't blame her brother, really. She'd messed up with her marriage pretty badly. But the solution was not to trade Gary's obsessive need to control her for Flint's obsessive protection, or any other man's. Her goal was to make it on her own, stand on her own two feet and show the world, herself and her son that she was done being a victim. Taylor McKade was a strong, independent woman.

"Nothing wrong with Flint wanting to take care of you and look out for you," Akeem was saying.

"Spoken like a true sheik."

He gave her an unreadable look. "What's that supposed to mean?"

"How many wives did your grandfather keep locked away in his harem?" she teased.

"I'm not my grandfather." His voice had an edge all of a sudden.

It made her do a double take. Touchy

subject? "I know. I didn't mean that." She stopped and set the briefcases down to rest her arms for a second. "You never talk about him."

He shrugged and dropped the sagebrush. They were coming into an area that was all stone and little dirt, the track barely visible this close up. Nobody would be able to pick it out from a helicopter. They were safe unless the police brought dogs. "He's dead." His voice was toneless.

"Flint says you refused your inheritance."

He said nothing to that, just swung both duffel bags over his right shoulder and picked up the two briefcases with the left and began walking again.

"I didn't mean to—"

"He didn't have a harem," he said. "He had four wives, each with their own kids in their own tent."

"Didn't you think that was strange when you were there?"

"Everything was strange. The wives were the least of it. I was born and raised in Houston. Not much here prepared me for the Bedu of the desert."

She hadn't known him back then. Neither had Flint. But he'd told her the few stories he'd heard from Akeem, back in the days when she had her first serious crush on him and had endlessly nagged her brother for every bit of information about his mysterious friend.

Akeem was fourteen when his mother died, no other relatives in the States. He would have gone into the foster-care system if not for his grandfather, the sheik, who had sent for him. He'd told Flint once that he had almost refused to go. It'd been hard for him to swallow that the old sheik had cast out his mother.

"Was it like this?" She nodded toward the barren land that surrounded them.

"Much bigger. In some places it's all stones, other places it's brush like this, even grass, then there are vast areas with nothing but sand. No TV, no video games. It was a shock to my fourteen-year-old system at first."

"And then?"

"And then I started to see the beauty of it, the honor of the men of the desert. I'd never seen the place before, but I still felt a connection." He shook his head. "Can't explain it. It was like… The best I can explain is collective memory."

"But you came back."

"First chance I got." He gave a lopsided smile. "I'm American."

He was unlike any man she had ever known: strong, honorable, carried himself with dignity, had always been there for the others. Flint considered him his brother, more so than the half brother they shared and hated discussing. Like Flint, Akeem had achieved great success. But sometimes she wondered if he ever felt at home anywhere.

She hadn't. Not in a long time. Not even at the ranch, despite the best efforts of Flint and Lora Leigh and Lucinda.

They walked on in silence, stopping only to drink. Akeem had brought along several bottles. Hopefully enough to last them until tomorrow.

Tomorrow, she would get Christopher back. She had to believe that.

They sat out the noon heat under a group of acacia trees and talked about his business. When the temperature cooled to bearable, they resumed walking again. They stopped for the night early, could have walked more given the light but decided it was better to save some energy for the next day. Who knew what it would require of them?

She helped him pitch the tent. They ate cold rations of smoked meat, bread and apples, courtesy of Lucinda, then drank sparingly.

"Should we light a fire?" she asked, not that it was that cold yet, but might get chilly toward dawn. Unless, by some miracle, Flint found them. He would be looking if they didn't get back to the ranch in a couple of hours.

"Better not."

Which meant, heaven help her, that they were going to have to snuggle for heat. She wasn't sure she was ready for that.

Okay, so she'd thought she'd been ready back when she was seventeen, when Akeem had first come home from Aggie, Texas A&M

University, with Flint on a visit. He'd starred in the overwhelming majority of her girlhood fantasies. Which culminated on that fateful night at nineteen when she'd been so summarily rejected.

The whirling sound of a helicopter interrupted the flow of memories before they could have made her blush.

AKEEM WATCHED AS TAYLOR cocked her head, her blond hair falling in waves over her shoulder.

"Police?" she asked.

"Either that or one of Jackson's choppers, or Flint's Falcon. We shouldn't call attention to ourselves until we know for sure."

The tent was small and a nondescript beige color that blended into the desert like camouflage. There were bushes around that were bigger. They had a fair chance that they might be mistaken for another boulder from a distance.

But as the chopper dipped low to scan the flat land, it did come to hover right on top of them. Akeem looked through the mosquito netting of the window. "Cops."

"Oh, man."

He waited for them to set down, trying to figure out what to say. They were about to catch some serious trouble for not telling the authorities about the ransom demand, for coming here alone. And they'd be summarily taken out of Hell's Porch, questioned for as long as the cops saw fit. When the next call could come at any second.

Akeem swore under his breath and got up. He would grab one of Flint's pickups and bring Taylor back here as soon as they were let go again. It was the best they could do; no point in wasting energy on what-ifs.

But after a moment of lingering in place, the chopper banked to the left and took off. His instincts prickled.

"Why didn't they stop to pick us up?" She came over to the window to look after the helicopter.

He ran his tongue over his teeth. Good question. Plenty of flat land to put the bird down. Why hadn't there been a more concentrated rescue effort, for that matter? And back at the boulders, why had the choppers attacked without waiting for ground support to get there?

It'd looked almost as if their purpose had been to bust up the exchange rather than to capture anyone or save Christopher. Just like right now their purpose seemed to be to locate Taylor and him, but not actually rescue them. Odd.

"You think they'll come back?"

Damned if he knew. If they had wanted to help or harm, they could have done it already.

"Let's move on." He was picking up the sleeping bag, not wanting to waste time.

"We just got settled in."

"I don't like this."

"I don't want to move."

He could more than understand. She had to be sore and exhausted.

"Just a couple of miles. We'll find someplace where we can spend the night without being visible from above."

"What if we lose the tracks in the twilight? We could end up going in the wrong direction." That panicked determination was back in her eyes again, like it had been during the firefight.

He understood. She was afraid that what-ever decision they made might turn out to be the wrong one for Christopher. She was holding up admirably, all in all. She had every right to be worried and emotional.

"If we get off track, it'll only be by a short distance. We can backtrack tomorrow. It's a chance we'll have to take," he said.

"Because of one lousy chopper?"

"Because if they weren't here to rescue us, then why were they here? Who needs our location? The location of the money." He stuffed his gear back into the duffel bags, leaving the small tent for last.

She watched him quietly. And after a moment, she moved to help.

She'd been right, he thought an hour later as they walked northeast, the direction the pickup had seemed to be heading, judging by the tracks. Tracks he hadn't seen for the past five minutes. If the ground had been muddy, or made of soft sand, the twilight would have been enough to pick out the tire tracks. Instead, the area was a combination of dirt and small rocks, the shallow impression the tires had made difficult enough to follow even in full light. They were losing the trail.

So he made a point in not going too far, not looking for the perfect place, just the nearest clump of acacias that was large enough and thick enough to hide the tent. Another ten minutes brought just such a stand of trees and bushes into view, but another half an hour passed before they reached it.

They set up the tent in silence. The leaves above filtered what little light was left.

He didn't understand how the cops had found them in the vast desert with such unerring certainty. It was as though the chopper had been headed straight to their tent. And how had they found them in the first place, at the boulder?

Even if Gary had tipped them off to the exchange, Gary hadn't known where exactly the exchange would take place. Taylor had been given that information little by little, over the phone the kidnappers had left for them. There had to be a locator. He hadn't found one in the Thermos, and in any case, the Thermos was no longer with them. Chances were that the locator had been someplace else all along.

He went still with the thought. "Come over here."

THE TENT WAS SMALL and dim, and she didn't know what he wanted from her, but she was too emotionally exhausted to worry about it.

"If the tracker wasn't in the Thermos Gary gave you, did he touch you?" His voice was slightly off.

"He gave me a hug when he showed up." And she'd been so relieved that he was sober and cooperating that she had let him that close, if only for a second.

"He could have planted a tracker on you then." Akeem was already reaching for her collar, running his sure fingers across the material, the back of his hand brushing the sensitive skin on her neck. "I don't want to turn on the flashlight in case anyone is out there looking for us. We can check by feel."

That Gary would betray her like this when their son's life was at stake defied belief. She stood still for the search, seething with anger.

Until Akeem's fingers brushed against her collarbone.

She held her breath.

When he didn't find anything there, he moved on, giving her clothing a thorough examination, down her arms, her waist, her legs to the cuffs on her pants, leaving a tingling path in his wake. But since stripping out of her clothes was the only alternative, she couldn't very well protest, not even if he was awakening some long-dormant sensations that made it difficult to remain motionless under his hands.

She felt nineteen again, except that she no longer needed beer in her system to dull her inhibitions. She was a grown woman. A woman who could still remember how she had thrown herself at Akeem, had touched him, pulled him close, had pressed her lips to his. She had wanted him with all the passion and desperation of youth.

And she wanted him still.

The realization came as a surprise, leaving her annoyed and embarrassed. And aching for more of his touches. But no way would she ever proposition him like that again. She'd just as soon not repeat the most embarrassing night of her life.

He'd shown little interest in her then, and even less since. Well, ever, to be truthful. And then there was Kat Edwards, the woman Akeem had not long ago brought out to the ranch. He'd asked Flint to hire her as a favor. And he'd been checking in with Flint on how she was doing. Who was she, and what was the relationship between the two? The few times Akeem visited lately, his first trip was always to Kat.

She had tried hard not to hate the woman who'd succeeded at getting Akeem's attention in a way she'd never been able to.

Even now, with him touching her and her body fairly begging for more, he was nothing if not professional, didn't linger. Her face, on the other hand, was flooded with heat by the time he finished. She was more than aware of his proximity, of the intimacy of their situation.

He stayed still for a long moment, breathed in, breathed out. "I can't find anything," he said darkly, then stood in front of her and held his arms out to the sides. "You're next. I've been talking to the cops. One of them could have stuck something on me while I was busy with the other."

An invitation to touch Akeem.

Oh, my.

What wouldn't she have given for this a couple of years back? And even now, she wasn't nearly as unaffected as she would have hoped. So much for all the maturity and self-control age was supposed to bring.

"So Kat is doing well at the ranch." Her hands slightly trembled, which was ridiculous. She reached for his collar before he could have noticed, determined to be just as matter-of-fact about all of this as he had been.

"She really likes it there," he said.

His shoulders were wide, his arms strong. She could feel the smooth bunch of muscles under his shirt, and pulled back a little before he thought she was copping a feel. Returning to a marginally more professional level, she checked the row of buttons on his shirt. *I can do this.* She almost had herself convinced when she looked up into his swirling dark eyes that seemed to shine in the dim tent.

There didn't seem to be any air in Hell's

Porch all of a sudden. The heat that filled the tent seemed to seep into her lungs and her blood.

"You two known each other long? I don't remember Flint mentioning her before." She pried for information.

"Friend of a friend."

And for some ridiculous reason, the unaffected way he said that made her happy in that moment.

He was as handsome as ever, and this was just about as close as they'd ever gotten. And he had to care about her, at least a little, to have come. Care about her or—

She leaned closer so she could identify the look in his dark eyes. *Oh, my.* She wasn't an inexperienced teenager anymore. She could tell when a man wanted her, and the look in Akeem's intense gaze was unmistakable.

Her heart thudded. Her fingertips tingled. Awareness stretched between them, making her mouth go dry.

Chapter Five

Akeem saw her eyes go wide, and his own need tried to make him think it was from desire. Common sense said it had to be alarm. His body burned for her. But the last thing he wanted to do was to make her feel uncomfortable, especially with all that was going on. She didn't need anyone putting the moves on her right now. She needed him to be a friend. She needed his support.

Pulling away was one of the hardest things

he'd done in his life, but he did it, then turned. "Check the back, then I can do the rest." If she touched him anywhere below the belt, he would have to work hard not to react.

"You have a gun?" she asked in a raspy voice after a moment, when her fingers found the weapon tucked into his waistband at the small of his back.

He hadn't realized that she hadn't seen it yet. "Problem?"

"No," came the single word from behind. "I'm glad you came prepared."

Prepared for a lot of things, but not for the way he was feeling right now. He didn't turn back to her—enough light remained for her to see exactly how much he wanted her.

He ran his hands along the seams of his pants to check for a transmitter. Swore when he found what he'd been looking for—a piece of black plastic the size of a fingernail. Someone had neatly dropped it into the cuff. Probably one of the cops, after Gary had told them that Akeem would be taking Taylor to the exchange.

"I'll go get rid of this then walk around to make sure there isn't something in the immediate vicinity we should know about." Like one of the kidnappers, or a stream of water, which he had yet to find during his Hell's Porch trips. There was rumor of a creek bed that held water, depending on the season.

Or a den of coyotes. He checked the gun.

He left her in the tent and circled their campsite in the last bit of light, doing his best to get his raging lust under control while he tried to pay attention to their surroundings. He saw nothing but more of the same of what they'd walked through to get here. He headed out then and threw the transmitter down a prairie-dog hole.

The sun had completely dipped below the horizon by the time he got back. Their sole sleeping bag was unzipped and spread out like a blanket. This way there was room for the both of them and neither would have to sleep on the bare ground. Taylor was lying on her side already. He zipped the tent flap behind him then lay down, leaving plenty of room between Taylor and himself when what he really wanted to do was draw her into his arms.

"Was everything okay?" she asked in the darkness.

"Not much out there."

She gave a soft sigh, and he knew she had hoped that he would discover something that would lead them to Christopher. And he wished he could have. More than anything, he wanted to see her and her son safe. He wanted to protect them from harm. Not just now, but forever. If only she'd give him a chance.

"We are not leaving here without him," he promised.

She drew a deep breath. "I'm sorry about—" She fell silent for a moment before continuing. "For kicking you at the boulder. You were protecting me. I'm glad that you are here."

He stared at the ceiling, not daring to look at her dim silhouette now that his eyes had gotten used to the dark of the tent. Lusting after her at a moment like this went beyond all propriety. He *was* here to protect and support her. "No problem."

"It is. I brought up your family in a way that was inexcusable. I don't really know anything about your family. I was a total jerk. You saved my life. I don't know what was wrong with me. I couldn't think of anything but Christopher."

"People say and do a lot of things they don't mean to when someone they love is threatened."

"I just went nuts."

He'd gone nuts, too, thinking she would go running into danger. He could understand. "Forget it. We're better friends than to let something like this be an issue between us."

Friends. Right. Except he was feeling anything but friendly at the moment. He settled in, knowing he hadn't much hope of falling asleep an arm's length from her, and from the way she was still fidgeting an hour later, he was pretty sure she wasn't asleep yet, either. He leaned toward her, not knowing even as he moved whether it was to make some light comment or draw her into his arms at last.

And they didn't find out, either. The buzz of a motor stopped him, the sound on the ground this time and not in the air, then another vehicle, coming from a distance.

The rumble of the engines was getting stronger.

"Who is that?" Taylor moved closer.

He had no answer. But whoever they were, they were heading toward the tent.

TAYLOR'S BREATH CAUGHT and all her senses focused, suddenly alert. *Please, God, don't let anything go wrong again.*

Akeem was sitting up already, shoving his feet back into his boots. "I'll check it out."

She didn't want to stay alone again in the dark tent. "I'll go with you."

He stood, held his hand out for her, his long fingers closing over her smaller ones in a firm, reassuring grip.

They zipped up the tent and kept low, in the cover of the sagebrush as they moved in the direction of the sound. Since visibility was decent in the moonlight, not much obstructing the view once they were out of the acacia patch, they didn't have to walk far before they spotted the small group of four-wheelers.

"Teenagers," Akeem whispered, although that precaution was probably unnecessary. Those kids wouldn't have heard him over the noise they were making.

He stayed down, and so did she as the kids did jumps over a rocky overhang. Wispy clouds drifted over the moon, then darker ones. Five minutes passed, ten, half an hour. The boys didn't seem to tire of their entertainment, not even when more clouds came, blocking out the moon. They didn't head out until the first drops of rain fell. So much for the weather forecasts.

By the time she and Akeem reached the tent, the rain was coming down hard, the noise of the four-wheelers fading in the distance.

She'd been soaked through. She tugged at her clothes, silently cursing the weather, not nearly as concerned about her wet clothes or the fact that, given enough rain, their tent could be washed away as she was about the tracks the rain was obliterating at this very moment.

"How will we find them?"

"Let's not worry about that until we see how bad things are in the morning. You better take those clothes off." Akeem's voice came from the dark. With the moon now under a cloud cover, virtually no light filtered into the tent. "You take the sleeping bag and wrap yourself up. I have an extra horse blanket in the bottom of the bag for emergencies."

She peeled off her shirt and pants and laid them out to dry at her feet then slipped into her sleeping bag. She nestled in, but couldn't get comfortable in the wet bra and underwear, so she tugged them off and carefully laid them next to her. Better. Except for the acute awareness that she was naked with Akeem.

At least he wasn't.

Then she heard the sound of wet clothes sliding against skin. And counted. Pants. Shirt. Socks. Then one more thing.

She whipped to her side, turning her back to him, and waited for her heart to slow. At least he didn't know that she was naked, too.

"If they don't dry by morning, they'll dry on us as soon as the sun comes up." His voice startled her.

Did he know? She pulled the sleeping bag to her chin.

"Don't worry. I can't see anything. Try to get some sleep."

Easy for him to say. She squirmed.

"Are you okay?"

Since she anticipated a lot more squirming before she would fall asleep, she needed to come up with an excuse to cover up how pitifully bothered she was by his nearness. His *naked* nearness.

"It's cold out here." She spoke nothing but the truth. The rain had brought the temperature down by twenty degrees in twenty minutes.

But apparently she had said just the wrong thing.

Akeem moved closer. "We can keep each other warm. Come on." He reached out in the darkness and pulled her to him, sleeping bag and all.

She froze, a full head-to-toe complete freak-out with her mind going blank. But when her brain began to function again, she did notice the heat that radiated from him, and how good that felt. Little by little, she allowed herself to relax against him, as much for his warmth as to prevent him from realizing how much his touch was affecting her.

And as if having her back resting against his broad chest wasn't enough, he placed his arm loosely on her waist and tucked her head under his chin.

"Goodbye, sleep," she mouthed silently into the darkness. But wouldn't have moved for anything.

THEY WERE MAKING slower progress than the day before, covering only ten miles or so by eleven. Akeem tried to shrug off his exhaustion. He hadn't slept much with Taylor in his arms. She'd been cold, but soft, a perfect fit, and soon enough her body had warmed to his. Then when she fell asleep and truly snuggled into him, curves against angles...

He hadn't been able to fall asleep until close to dawn. And now he was paying the price for it. But being able to hold Taylor in his arms was worth a sleepless night. It was worth so much more than that.

"Are you sure we're going the right way?" Taylor had walked a step or two behind him earlier in the morning to benefit from his shadow—little things like that could make a big difference in the desert—but with the sun now high in the sky, his shadow was negligible so they were walking beside each other.

"It's our best bet."

The rain had washed away the tracks from the day before, but they'd crossed a set of fresh ones that seemed very similar, heading in the same direction. His instincts said they were on the right path. He wondered if they were being followed.

Doing a full-body search of Taylor last night, he had nearly lost control. Those kids on four-wheelers had reminded him at the last second just how easily it could have been someone else, how vigilant he needed to remain. Not allowing any distractions.

He was going to help her find Christopher. Then he was going to figure out who was responsible for the kidnapping and take care of him. For good. The darkness rose inside him, but for once, he didn't care.

He would not stand for Taylor and her son being in danger. If necessary, he was going to put his own security in place to make sure something like this never happened again. And when she had settled back down to normal life, when she had some time to get over her divorce and all this, he would do his best to win her heart. His best friend's little sister or not, he couldn't let Taylor McKade slip away from him again. He was going to court her.

The notion sounded old-fashioned, but that was what he wanted. If he tried for a quick fling, Flint would kill him anyway. And he didn't want a quick fling. He wanted to spend time with her, to protect her, to have her fall in love with him. He wanted marriage, brothers and/or sisters for Christopher. He wanted forever with Taylor McKade.

But he would be the worst kind of man if he pushed her now, before she was ready. So he had held her through the night, giving her the sense of security and comfort she needed and not making a move, not touching her in any other way beyond that, even if his body had been as hard as the boulders that littered the landscape.

And he needed to think about something else, or he'd soon be back in the same condition all over again.

"How is the foot?" he asked.

She'd been limping slightly for the past couple of miles. Looked like her shoes were beginning to rub.

"Fine."

Of course, she would have said that no matter what. She had that stubborn look on her face. Nothing was going to stop Taylor McKade this time.

"Let's take a break and have a drink." The sun was nearing its zenith. No call so far.

She had worried that the kidnappers would delay too long and the battery might run out, leaving them without means to communicate. And truly lost in the desert. He'd checked the battery power the last time they had stopped. It had less than half of its life left.

"When we reach those boulders," Taylor said.

He squinted at the dark mass she was indicating in the distance. Made sense. They needed shade. But he would have preferred if she rested sooner. "Let me take those."

She was carrying the briefcases again. "I can handle it." She wouldn't even slow down.

The closer they got to the boulders, the more familiar they seemed, giving him some

hope at last. "I think I've been here before."
A couple of years back.

"You know where we are?"

"Near the center." He'd camped by these
boulders.

From time to time, when a strange loneli-
ness broke over him, he would come out here.
He missed his mother; he missed Beharrain,
even. He'd missed Taylor when she'd been
married to another man, and had been biding
his time, giving her some space to find sure
footing since her divorce.

Not that he had lived like a monk all his life.
Some of the same men who sneered at his
heritage would have been only too happy to
meld his auction house and millions into their
own holdings through marriage. There had
never been a shortage of introductions. But
as a rule, he'd never gone for the not-so-

innocent debutantes put in his path. For his rare affairs, he preferred women who knew the score. And from time to time, he was able to lose himself in them.

At other times, when he was sick of all that, he packed up some rations, vaulted his favorite black Arabian stallion and headed out to Hell's Porch. Being alone with nature wasn't the same as being lonely. The Arabian Desert and his uncles had taught him that.

And now he was here with Taylor. A damn strange turn of events.

An hour passed before they reached their destination.

"Let me see that." He took her feet in hand as soon as she sat on the smallest of the boulders, a pickup-size rock that on one end was only waist high.

"Taylor." He couldn't help the growl from his voice as he pulled off her sneakers and saw the bloody sock. "Why didn't you say something? I have bandages." He reached for the first-aid kit that had somehow worked its way to the bottom of the duffel bag.

"Sorry. Forgot about that. I just—" She raised her gaze to his.

And he understood. Her mind had been elsewhere. On her son. And she'd been in a hurry to get to him. "Let's see how bad it is." He peeled the sock back.

Her heel was raw, her feet small and dainty in his palms. She shouldn't be out in the middle of Hell's Porch. His anger intensified against the kidnappers. He gritted his teeth, forcing his focus away from that. There would be time when he caught up with the bastards.

He turned her foot over. Pale skin, a pronounced arch, perfect round toenails done in gold. He had to shake his head at that. "I'll do the best I can." The kit was fully stocked. He hadn't had occasion to use it much.

His first instinct was to wrap her up and take her to safety, away from all danger, to protect her, to take care of her. But he knew how much she hated it when Flint tried to do that.

"I *am* going to protect you," he told her, just so there'd be no confusion about what she should expect.

"Fine and dandy," she said, looking behind his back. Her flippant tone belied the way her face turned white for a second before she gathered herself. And the next moment, the corner of her eyes were crinkling with resolution, a slow smile tugging up one corner of her mouth. "But I'm going to have to protect you first. Don't move a muscle."

He froze. Not only because he, too, could now sense danger, but also because at this very moment she was the Taylor of old, before that bastard ex-husband of hers had come along. She was taking the situation in hand with her old self-assurance.

"Okay, you can move the muscle that's needed to slide your gun over."

He did as she asked. She didn't look like she was joking.

"Notice how I'm trusting you," he said.

"What? I don't have trust issues."

"Mmm, hmm."

She fitted in a glare before she raised the gun and took off the safety. Flint had taught her how to shoot. Even Akeem had done some target practice with her back in the day. He had no worries there.

They were both still and silent. He was about to ask what she was doing when he heard the rattler's warning, coming no more than inches from his back.

TAYLOR HAD A CLEAR view of the rattler's head. She would get one chance only. She needed to shoot a bullet an inch over Akeem's shoulder as he held his body half-bent to her foot, aim an inch from his left ear.

Knowing she could do it and actually pulling the trigger were two different things, however.

"I trust you," he said again in that steady, sure voice of his.

God, she had missed that voice. She hated what their friendship had become. Hated that she'd been the one to ruin it with that stupid crush of hers. He'd been staying away from her, and lately away from the ranch because of her.

But now he was here.

And keeping him here—alive—was up to her.

She closed her left eye, lined up the target and pulled the trigger.

The force of the bullet punched the snake back a couple of paces. She looked at the writhing, bloody mess on the stone behind Akeem and shivered.

"I'm glad I can still do this." She set the gun down with trembling hands, as all bravado was leaving her.

Akeem straightened, looked back to the snake before turning again to her. "You mean you haven't been practicing lately?"

"Not since Christopher was born. Not enough time to do everything in a day."

He made some noise, then, with a strange look in his eyes, stepped around her.

Probably needed to walk off the tension. But he stopped abruptly.

"Taylor?" he asked from behind her, then turned her before she had a chance to turn on her own.

His tanned hands held her by the shoulders. The focused look that had been in his eyes before morphed into swirling dark heat. She barely had time to catch her breath before he hauled her up, dipped his head and kissed her.

Slow. Tender. Thorough.

Oh, my.

Akeem Abdul never did anything halfway, at least that was what they said about him in the business arena, and she was getting her chance to find out firsthand.

His lips brushed over hers, warmed them, caressed, nibbled. She opened to him without thought, slipping into her girlhood fantasies. Oh, but reality was so much better than anything she could have imagined.

She felt as if she'd been made for this man's mouth, for this man's arms. She gave herself over to the kiss, to oblivion, to Akeem. He tasted her over and over again, claimed her. Branded her. Her body flooded with pleasure. Which he ended too soon.

"Sorry." He squeezed his eyes shut for a moment, ran his thumb over his left eyelid. "I mean, thank you." He looked endearingly frazzled when his eyes opened. "Sorry about the kiss. Thank you for the snake," he clarified as he stepped back.

She was about to tell him that he could drop the sorry part, when the phone rang. Fear spiked through her, instantly erasing the last of the pleasant sensations that still lingered.

"Are you ready to pay attention this time?" the voice asked when she opened the cell phone and pressed it to her ear.

THE SECOND EXCHANGE attempt had been set up at a rock formation one mile east of the original, for the next morning. Except that they were marching in the opposite direction.

Taylor kept her eyes on the ground as she walked behind Akeem, keeping in his shade as he had instructed. "Are you sure about this?"

"Not nearly sure enough, but it's the best chance we have at this stage. I'm pretty sure the pickup tracks that we've been following were leading us to the closed-down refinery that's out this way."

The refinery her grandfather had worked at

one point in his life. She'd heard tales about that, but had never been all the way out here. There were far more pleasant places to ride around Flint's ranch.

Unfortunately, the whirling gusts of wind that had swept through after lunch had obliterated the pickup tracks.

"I've ridden through here before. I should be able to find the refinery by instinct," Akeem told her. They could have been going around in circles, for all she knew. She'd become disoriented a while back. She was filled with doubts and she hated every one of them.

Taylor put one foot in front of the other, trying her best to trust him, but trust didn't come easily to her. She'd trusted Gary so innocently, so thoroughly. Then he had turned into a monster she no longer knew. And then he had hurt her.

Maybe, if she was the only person at stake, she could trust Akeem more fully. Maybe. But her son… She couldn't trust Christopher to anyone just yet. Not after she had trusted him to Jake Kenner. Because Jake had been one of Flint's men and Flint always treated his employees as family and they had always loved him back and had been fiercely loyal. All but Jake.

She had gotten lulled into a false sense of security, thinking she'd be safe because she'd gotten away from Gary and she was with Flint. But Christopher hadn't been safe. She couldn't make that mistake again.

Tomorrow, the voice had said.

Which meant that Christopher would have to spend one more night with those criminals. Almost another whole day in which anything could happen. She could hardly bear the thought; it wrung her heart out, leaving her empty.

"Why are they making us wait? This is driving me crazy," she snapped.

"That's why," Akeem said without turning. "They want you scared and compliant this time. They probably figure we can't have many resources left. They prefer us hungry and dehydrated."

"Weak," she said, summing it up. She did feel that already, listlessness interspersed with periods of murderous rage that someone would do this to her son. That rage gave her the energy to go on.

Although Akeem had come prepared, he hadn't expected to spend days in Hell's Porch. They had one bottle of mineral water left between the two of them, and at least another twenty-four hours to go. If they were lucky. If they were going in the right direction.

She didn't know how she could possibly put all her hopes in the hands of Akeem Abdul, a man she'd barely seen in the past couple of years. But a man she knew to be true and good, nevertheless, she reminded herself.

She wasn't going to think about what it had felt like to spend the night in his strong arms. Not now.

His skin was soft, stretched over hard muscles that came from hard riding. Akeem was a formidable horseman, and he'd seen her at Flint's plenty of times with the wild mustangs Flint bought from the government each year to introduce to his breeding program.

His lean but powerful thighs had been pressed against the back of hers for most of the night and—

Good thing she hadn't yet known how well the man could kiss.

So much for not thinking about him. She bit back a groan, looked up at the sun and wiped her sweat-beaded forehead. "The heat is definitely back today." The cooling effect of last night's rain was long gone, the ground as dry as if it had never happened, the only sign of recent moisture the plants that stood straighter and looked greener than the day before.

"We'll stop for another break soon. The refinery shouldn't be more than a couple of hours from here," he said.

But he was wrong.

Either he'd remembered in riding distance—much faster than walking—or they were seriously slowing down due to their insufficient rations of food and water. The sun was ready to retire for the day by the time they rounded a dip in the landscape and came upon a higher point and she could see the refinery up ahead in a shallow bowl of rock and sand.

The complex looked deserted, no vehicles in sight. No sign of life whatsoever, no matter how carefully she looked, eyes squinted, her hand over her brows to block the sun.

Her heart dropped to the bottom of her grumbling stomach.

They had gambled everything on Akeem's hunch. If they'd made a mistake by coming here, Christopher was in big trouble. Because there was no way to get back to the kidnapper's assigned meeting point by tomorrow morning.

"Keep low." Akeem crouched to stay below the waist-high brush that covered most of the landscape.

She followed his example, and another hour passed before they reached the first fence. Her thigh muscles were about ready to explode. Walking in a crouch for this long had put the worst boot camp–style exercise program to shame. "And now?"

"We go in and look around." He was already moving toward a spot where a clump of larger bushes had grown close against the fence. He was unraveling the chain link by the time she caught up with him.

They squeezed through only to realize that the second fence was much sturdier than the first, with barbed wire on top and EPA notices every hundred feet or so warning everyone to keep out. The strip between the two fences had scarce vegetation, not much to hide behind. Anyone from the refinery could see them if they were looking.

Akeem signaled toward what looked like a beat-up guardhouse. He walked over, peeked in through the glassless window before going in.

"What are we doing here?" She followed him and closed the door carefully behind her.

"Waiting for the night to get a little darker. Getting some rest. Giving anyone who might be in there—" he indicated the refinery "—time to fall asleep." He shrugged off the duffel bags, banged around a little to scare the snakes and scorpions out, then sat.

She did the same. Her shoulders and back ached from carrying the two briefcases all day. Even her blisters had blisters. The muscles in her legs throbbed. She was an active person, but her job required her to spend considerable time behind a desk. She hadn't been on a multiday hike since Christopher had been born. Riding out to the south pasture once or twice a week hadn't prepared her for this. She hoped Christopher was here, because she wasn't sure how much farther she could go.

She pushed that thought aside. Nonsense. She would walk as far as necessary, even to the ends of the earth.

Akeem watched her as she stretched her fingers, then tightened them into a fist a couple of times, then rolled her shoulders. "Sore?"

"I'm so far past sore, I can't even remember it. I think my muscles have set themselves on fire in protest."

He smiled in the dim space, leaned against the wall, spread his legs. "Come over here."

Her heart beat out a staccato rhythm.

The awareness was back between them with full force, and she wondered for a moment if this would always happen when they were in close proximity. Heaven help her if it did.

He waited.

She gave up pretending that she could have resisted.

When she scooted over to him, he turned her and pulled her closer. She would have been grateful for a reassuring hug, for the slightest offer of comfort. But he placed his long fingers on her shoulders and began to work them. For the first second or two, all she felt was more pain, then she relaxed as tension leaked out when he pressed the heel of his hand against her spine.

"God, that feels good. Where did you learn to do that?" He was a surprise and a half. Akeem Abdul, prince of the desert, as a trained masseur?

"Horses," he said behind her.

Of course. She rolled her eyes, a smile tugging at the corner of her lips. He was treating her like a horse. But she wouldn't have moved an inch. What he was doing felt way too wonderful.

When he was done with her neck, he moved to her shoulders, then to her back, her lower back, then back up again to her arms. Tingles galore. When he was done with the arms, he turned her sideways in the bracket of his legs.

She was really hoping for a kiss. Pitifully so. But instead, he took her left hand, worked through each individual finger, joint by joint, then her palm. When he was done, he did the right hand. "Lie down," he said after that.

She did so, thinking they would be going to sleep, getting ready to fight down the heat that had spread through her body, to ignore the needs he'd awakened inside her. But instead of lying down to rest, he positioned himself at her feet.

Oh.

She wasn't sure if she could handle that. "You don't have to— I don't think—"

He was kneading her calf muscles already. "We have a big day tomorrow. If your muscles stiffen up and you can't move when you have to, or if you can't move fast enough…."

He didn't have to finish the sentence. She let go of all feelings of embarrassment over the fact that she was melting in his hands and gave herself over to the feel of his long fingers moving up her legs. She could feel the warmth of his hands through the fabric of her pants, and desire soon raced across her skin.

He was silhouetted in the moonlight, on his knees before her, leaning over her. She closed her eyes, meant to turn her head to the side but ended up arching her neck instead and even perhaps her back, too, as his hands moved above her knees.

She didn't think he noticed, but when he stopped a few minutes later and asked, "Feeling better?" his voice was dangerously raspy.

The air was thicker than Houston at a hundred percent humidity, and they were in the desert. The guardhouse seemed to be getting smaller by the minute.

"Mmm, hmm," she said, then realized how pitiful that sounded and gathered all her strength for a "Thank you."

She should have probably returned the favor; his muscles had to be hurting as much as hers. But for once, she was smart enough to know when to stop. No way she could have touched him and not made a complete fool of herself. So she simply pulled aside to make more room for him on the floor.

He stretched out next to her and came up on

his left elbow. "You look beautiful in the moonlight."

Which was so not what she needed to hear. They would both have been much better off if he'd said something like her feet smelled. Too much touching, too much intimacy had filled the tiny place. They needed to neutralize that before one of them did something stupid. Okay, before she did something stupid. Because, God help her, she was on the verge of begging him to kiss her again and make her forget all the danger around them and the situation they were in, make her forget just for a night.

But she'd done the begging before. And he had said no and walked away. And she had sworn that if she survived the embarrassment, she was never going to do anything as stupid as that ever again.

"I think tomorrow—" She started into a random thought, having no idea what she was going to say next.

Which didn't turn out to be a problem.

Akeem's lips sealed hers long before she could have gotten to the end of the sentence.

Firm. Warm. Coaxing.

Surprise made her stiffen, but only for a moment. Her body took over next. She tasted him first, which surprised him in turn. His dark eyes flared with heat.

Fantasies that were nearly a decade old came back in full force as his dark eyes closed and his chest expanded under her palm. They were close enough for her to feel his body harden with desire. The thought that she had caused that surprised her again and aroused her at the same time.

Then some sort of Texas tornado formed

inside the guardhouse and blew their clothes clear off before she even knew what was happening, leaving her in her bra and underwear, and Akeem in dark gray boxer shorts. She couldn't remember touching a single button, yet the speed with which their pants had been divested indicated that she had helped.

All she knew were Akeem's lips on hers, tasting her, demanding entry, his palm closed over her breast, her mind melting under the onslaught of desire.

His long fingers caressed her skin, heating her flesh further, melting her at her core as she arched her back. He immediately took advantage and sealed his lips around her sensitized nipple, with nothing but some flimsy lace between them. Her blood sang as it pulsed through her body.

It seemed crazy, but after all her wanderings, in that dilapidated guardhouse in the middle of Hell's Porch, when she was in Akeem's arms, she felt like she had found home at last.

Chapter Six

Going slowly had been his mantra over the past few months when it came to Taylor. That resolution was flying out the glassless window with racehorse speed.

She was practically naked, and she was perfect. Beyond perfect. She was so beautiful it made his throat tighten. She was Taylor. Taylor McKade was in his arms. How long had he waited for this?

A century would have been worth every minute.

She needed distraction, just one moment in the midst of all danger and worry. He needed her, plain and simple. But this wasn't going to be about him.

He wanted her to feel sheltered. Better yet, transported. And just good, plain good. As good as she was making him feel.

Taylor was in his arms and she was kissing him.

Getting carried away would have been the easiest thing in the world to do. So he made sure she was on board with every move he made. And he was eager to make as many moves as their limited time would allow.

He caressed her breasts first, breasts that had grown fuller with motherhood. Her nipples tightened against his palm. The exquisite sensation pumped heated blood through his veins. And things only got hotter when he pulled his lips from hers and bent to take a nipple into his mouth through her yellow lace bra.

Yellow lace was going to be the death of him yet.

His hand slipped down her flat stomach, her hip, the outside of her lean thigh. Her skin was soft and smooth. He reveled in the feel of it as he hooked a hand under her knee and pulled the leg up. He wanted nothing more than to lose himself in her body and make her come apart in his arms.

On some level, he was aware that he wasn't thinking, but he couldn't bring himself to start. Feeling was so incredibly good. Who needed thoughts?

He soaked up the feel of her as her knees parted to let him closer.

"Are you sure?" He pressed against her core, leaving no doubt what he was asking.

She opened those cornflower eyes that looked midnight blue in the dark, and fixed her gaze on him. "Of course I'm not sure."

And in an instant their circumstances came back to his mind again. Thoughts cranked into gear even as his body protested. He had sought to make her forget for a while, and instead it had been him who had forgotten just about everything. A car door slamming outside underscored the realization. He hadn't even heard the vehicle roll up.

He swore and came up to a crouch to spy through the window. One of the pickups from the day before was standing in front of the gate no more than thirty feet from the guardhouse.

One man got out. He had a key to the padlock.

It wasn't Jake Kenner, but definitely one of the guys who'd been there at the boulder.

The man got into the vehicle, rolled through the inner gate then got out to lock it again. Akeem yanked his pants on and pushed the door open, waited until the man was coming back to his pickup, not ten feet from the guardhouse. When the guy was close enough, Akeem rushed forward without a weapon. He needed both hands free.

The heightened emotions that had filled him just moments ago switched to determination and anger in a split second. This was the bastard who had taken Christopher. He felt his control snap, felt that Bedu warrior blood in his veins that he'd been hiding all his life. And this time, he didn't care.

He brought the man to the ground, one hand going to the guy's mouth, the other to hold him down. The bastard bit hard, to the bone, and in a reflex response, Akeem's hold loosened. Only for a second, but that was enough. The man pulled a knife and embedded it in Akeem's thigh.

Pain seared down his leg, but Akeem didn't let go. He hauled the bastard up and kept the pickup between himself and the refinery, for cover, as he dragged the man back to the guardhouse with him, each step hurting like a sonofabitch. He had his own knife stuck in the back of his waistband, but his hands weren't free to reach for it.

"You raise your voice, you die. Now, where's the kid?" he asked when he had the guy inside and hauled up against the wall. He kept his weight on his good leg as he loosened his hand around the guy's mouth, keeping the bastard's neck pinned with his other arm.

Akeem had him opposite the window so a slice of moonlight lit the guy. Looking into that shifty face filled him with anger. He and his partners in crime had taken an innocent little boy, shattered the child's sense of safety probably for years or decades to come, for something as inconsequential as money. They might as well have ripped the heart from Taylor's chest. And Akeem found that he knew no mercy when it came to someone hurting Taylor or her son.

Pain pulsed through him, honing his anger to a fine edge. "This is the last time I'm going to ask nicely. Where's the kid?"

The man was glancing around, hoping to spot a possible weapon or a way out, no doubt. He didn't understand the severity of his situation. He lurched against Akeem's hold. "Who the hell—"

"Wrong answer." He smacked the guy's head against the wall. "Where is Christopher?"

They were running out of time. He reached for his gun on the small desk in the corner, pressed the barrel under the man's chin, although he had no intention of shooting this close to their target and alerting everyone. Since the guy was here, he was even more sure now that they had to be keeping something valuable at the refinery. Most likely they were hiding Christopher somewhere here. But the buildings were enormous. He needed to know where to go and where the traps lay that he needed to avoid.

At this moment, he was willing to do anything to get that information.

The man he'd captured didn't have much of a choice. He had to know that he would either talk and be killed by his buddies when they caught up with him, or not talk and meet a bad end right now, right here. Akeem pressed his arm harder into his Adam's apple and watched dispassionately as he gasped for air.

And as he waited for the guy's head to turn purple, for some indication from him that he'd made his decision, he realized that Taylor hadn't made a sound since he had come back inside. He knew what she must be seeing: him turned into a murderous animal, the violence of his true temperament showing at last. A quick glance sideways at her wide-eyed faced confirmed his thoughts.

But it had been a mistake to look. The guy dropped his weight and twisted out of Akeem's grasp, grabbing for the knife still embedded in Akeem's thigh and making him see stars as he yanked it. That split second, while Akeem caught his breath in the middle of the searing pain, was enough for the guy to throw himself at Taylor, the nasty-looking knife back in his hand.

The balance of power shifted as easily as that.

"Tell me where the boy is and you can go. I have no argument with you." Akeem dropped the gun, but not in capitulation. He needed to free his right hand.

"Get out of my way," the man growled, pressing the tip of his knife to Taylor's throat.

Akeem watched as a bead of blood formed, then ran down her pale neck. The trail of blood looked black in the dark.

Rage filled him, more powerful than anything he had felt before. Rage that pushed him to act without thought. And that was dangerous. So he tempered it to cold anger as he locked eyes with the man. And realized that the guy wasn't about to negotiate. He clearly thought he had the upper hand, especially with his buddies nearby to back him up. Depending on where they were in the refinery, they might or might not hear a shout in the night.

The man was already opening his mouth. More blood ran down Taylor's neck. She stood completely still, without so much as a whimper, her gaze locked on Akeem's.

And he realized that he really had no choice. He brought his own knife from his back the next second and threw it with enough force to embed it in the man's windpipe, with only the handle sticking out, a skill he'd learned from his uncles in the desert on their gazelle-hunting trips.

Then he grabbed for Taylor and yanked her from the man before blood spurted from behind the base of the knife's handle. The kidnapper folded soundlessly to the ground.

When Taylor tried to turn and look, Akeem held her to him and pressed her face into the crook of his neck, his body awash in adrenaline. "Go to the pickup. Get in on the passenger side. Get down. Don't look back." He wouldn't let her go until she nodded against him.

He positioned himself between her and the body on the floor anyway, and waited until she was out before turning to pick up his shirt. He ripped off one sleeve to make a tight bandage around his thigh, the other to wrap up the bleeding bite on his hand.

Damn.

He drew a deep breath when he was done, his blood calming as he looked over the dead man. "Who the hell are you?" His gaze locked on eyes that stared into eternity.

Then he thought of Taylor.

He hated that she'd had to see this.

For him, it was different. Wasn't the first time. Not that it got better or easier. He'd shot a man at sixteen in the Arabian Desert in self-defense. His grandfather had insisted on taking him to a tribal skirmish. To make a man out of him, the old sheik had said.

And made him fear just what kind of man he would become.

Now he knew. And so did Taylor.

He drew a slow breath, telling himself he needed to get moving, yet hesitating for another moment. When he had talked the kidnappers into letting him come along, he had known things might come to this. That was specifically why he was here, to protect Taylor and Christopher at any cost, even at the cost of human life, even if that life were his own.

Still, he couldn't bring himself to take his

knife back. He grabbed the attacker's blade from the floor instead, then patted him down. No other weapon. He'd probably left his gun in the pickup when he got out to lock the inner gate behind him and open the outer one so he could leave. No identification. He pocketed the man's cell phone, swore under his breath, pried up the floorboards in the corner then hid the duffel bags and briefcases after having grabbed a handful of items from the first-aid kit. Then he picked up the guy's baseball hat and shoved it onto his own head before heading for the pickup.

"You okay?" were his first words when he got in and saw Taylor bent over to keep down. "How bad is your neck?" He couldn't see from this angle.

"Just a scratch." She straightened in her seat. "You?" She was watching him carefully.

Warily? He couldn't see well enough in the dark to tell.

He remembered Carolyn all of a sudden. *"I just don't feel safe around you. I'm sorry."* She'd fidgeted across the table from him at one of Houston's most expensive restaurants. It had been just after 9/11. He hadn't bothered to discuss the issue. She hadn't been that important to him. He had stood and walked away. But Taylor *was* important to him. He didn't want her to be afraid of him. He grabbed the dead man's gun from the dashboard and shoved it into his waistband, next to his own, out of sight.

"No damage." He wanted to check her neck, to treat it, to see the full extent of the injury, but he didn't want to turn on the light in the cab, in case someone was watching from a window somewhere. There'd been enough funny business going on around the guardhouse to draw suspicion if someone was paying attention.

But so far, nobody had raised an alarm. Maybe they thought themselves safe and were resting up for the exchange in the morning.

Taylor glanced back to the guardhouse. "Now there's one less of them. And we know they are definitely using this place for something."

Her voice was strained, but she wasn't falling apart, and he was grateful for that. Then grateful yet again to spot a half-dozen keys on the chain that hung from the ignition. He pulled the truck forward to the gate along the inner fence, ignoring the Posted and Illegal Entry signs, then took the key ring to try his luck with the padlock.

The first key didn't fit. Neither did the

second. If someone looked out from one of the buildings, they would definitely be able to tell that Akeem was not the guy they'd expected.

He glanced toward the pickup. Taylor was watching him. He should have told her to get back down again.

He tried another key, and that one slid in at last, turned in the lock. They were riding through toward the refinery complex within seconds. He kept the headlights turned off.

"Have you been to this place before?" she asked, taking stock of their surroundings.

"Once."

"Inside?"

"Rode around it. I was camping not far from here for a couple of days."

He kept an eye on the structures for any sign of danger as he navigated between two large pits then two brick tanks, driving toward the main tower and the utility building. The place looked ready to fall apart. He said as much to Taylor.

"They closed it up in 1980. My grandfather worked here for a while."

"No kidding?" He glanced at her. "So you know this place?"

"Just heard the tales. Can't be that many old oil refineries out here. Grandpa said they used to make roofing tar. His team, anyway."

"He tell you anything else?"

"Not much. He hadn't worked out here that long. Had a falling-out with the boss over an accident his best friend was involved in."

He kept going, hoping to spot some other vehicles and figure out where the men were. Nothing. He drove slowly to keep the engine quiet as he weaved among the various structures, some of which looked like they might be ready to collapse at any second.

Long minutes had passed by the time he caught sight of two pickups—same as he was driving—parked under what looked like a covered loading dock.

Taylor leaned forward, gripping the dashboard as she peered ahead. She was growing more tense with every passing second. Then, when he turned off the car, she whispered a question. "Do you think he's here?"

"We got three out of the five pickups. Sure looks like mission headquarters to me." He wouldn't let his concern over the two missing vehicles show.

She was plenty nervous already. And deep in thought.

He was about to get out when she drew her shoulders up, took a deep breath then went completely still the next second. Only her lips moved as she said, "I want you to leave me here."

"In the pickup?" Might not be a bad idea. As long as she kept down. She might be safer in the vehicle while he looked around out there.

But she was shaking her head, a tone of desperation creeping into her voice. "I want you to take this car and go back."

At first, he couldn't comprehend what she meant. Then he understood only too well. She had seen what he'd done at the guard-house and she no longer felt comfortable around him. Hell, maybe she no longer felt *safe* around him. One thing was certain—she no longer wanted his help.

Being pushed away by her hurt more than his combined injuries. "You need me here," he argued. "You might not like who I am, but

I'm what you need." If she thought she was going to calmly waltz in and negotiate with those guys, she was more naïve that he'd judged her to be. "This is what it's going to come down to, Taylor. Violence. You don't have to like it, but you're going to have to let me handle it, because there's no way in hell I'm leaving you and Christopher behind."

He grabbed her arm without thinking, then dropped it when he caught himself. "No way in hell."

HE COULD BE STUBBORN, but so could she. "He's my son. This is my problem. I want you to go."

Even in the middle of the night, the moon provided enough light for her to see his blood-soaked leg. He needed help.

At one point along the way, she realized

that this wasn't going to be a simple exchange. People were going to get hurt. Akeem already had. People were going to die. Possibly her, but she could live with that. She was willing to go as far as she possibly could with this, no matter the end. She would get her son back or die trying.

She couldn't expect the same from Akeem. He wasn't Christopher's parent. Scorching kisses and some serious groping notwithstanding, he was nothing but a girlhood crush and her brother's friend.

"I didn't ask you to get involved in this," she snapped at him and watched the gathering storm on his face.

"Too damn bad," he said tight-lipped.

"You have nothing to do with us," she said in a fierce whisper.

His lips flattened into an even tighter line,

until they all but disappeared. A long second passed before he spoke, his voice low and hard. "Everything that happens to you concerns me, Taylor."

Her heart slammed against her chest.

She was trying to save him, didn't he understand? Apparently not, and it was probably a good thing, because if he did, there was no way in hell he would leave.

"Akeem, you—"

He cut her off. "What is your plan?"

"I go in and talk to them. With me alone and unarmed they won't feel threatened. I'll tell them where the money is." She paused. "I swear I'll pay you back." She ignored the look he shot her, and went on. "When they rush off to get the money, I'll take Christopher and hide somewhere in case they come back. But I don't think they will. They'll be running off with your millions."

It *could* work that way, not that she thought it would. Something didn't add up with the whole kidnapping. She fought to remain optimistic, but her instincts said to expect a darker end. And Akeem didn't need to be part of that.

"I'm coming with you every step of the way until you and Christopher are safely back at the ranch. It's your choice if you don't ever want to see me after that." His face was as hard as his voice.

Warning flashed in his eyes. He was spitting mad at her.

She didn't care. As long as he got away from this place in one piece and lived. "You have to—"

She couldn't finish once again. He grabbed for her and hauled her against him, taking her mouth in a kiss that was far from his previous gentle seductions. He took her this time, with or without her consent, making her powerless in his grip, in the swirl of sensations and emotions that washed over her, leaving her breathless.

"Tell me I have nothing to do with you," he growled when he let her go at last.

She couldn't have, even if she could talk.

The air was too charged with tension between them—sexual and every other kind—to properly draw a breath. She reached for the door handle instead, and got out on shaky legs.

Akeem was right behind her. And when in a few steps her stunned surprise wore off, all she could think of was that after all these years…

How dare he kiss her like that just when they were walking into death? She didn't know whether to tear into him for that or ask for another one.

At another time perhaps.

But she couldn't afford to think of anything else but her son right now, couldn't afford to spend much more time fighting Akeem off. She'd tried. She wished he had gone. But he was here, and he was going to have to take responsibility for his own choices.

Everybody did. That was one of the things she was learning.

"We are not just waltzing in there and hoping to negotiate," Akeem said as he passed her. "We'll go in without being seen and assess the situation then make a plan."

And she gave up fighting him any further, because, honestly, it was such a comfort and relief to have him there. She looked around and surveyed the surrounding area and buildings. No windows looked this way that she could tell. When they walked around the corner, they spotted a rusty metal door. She followed Akeem toward it.

Unfortunately, none of his keys opened the lock. She had a feeling the guy they'd gotten the keys from was supposed to call up and identify himself for someone to come down and let him in.

And since neither her nor Akeem's voice was one the people in there would recognize, it seemed they were officially out of luck.

They'd come pretty far against all odds. But now, an arm's reach from their goal, they were stuck. Out in the open with no way in and no place to hide if one of the two missing pickups pulled up.

"Do you think he was expected to come

back?" She was referring to the man who had nearly cut her neck.

"Probably. Most likely, they're following some sort of a plan."

"So someone will come outside to look for him at some point?"

"It'd make more sense for them to call his cell." He pulled a black phone from his pocket.

She hadn't realized they had another phone now. "Can I call Flint?"

He tossed her the phone. "You bet." The words were easily spoken, but his face remained dark. He hadn't forgiven her for trying to send him away.

But he hadn't raised his voice. Not once. Hadn't raised his hand. A different man from Gary altogether. There *were* different men. Not that she hadn't known that on an intellectual level. There was Flint, for example.

But Flint was her brother. Akeem was a whole other kind of experience.

She was dialing her brother's number already when she thought of something and her fingers went still, hovering above the keypad. "You don't think the phone might be monitored?"

"I don't see any reason why they should keep track of their own calls."

"Good." She pressed the call button, and said, "It's me, Taylor" as soon as the other end was picked up. "Are you alone?"

"Are you okay?"

"Fine. We're at the old refinery where Gramps used to work. Christopher might be here."

"The cops are still downstairs. Want me to—"

"No."

"Jackson's pilots are here, too. We've been grounded by the police. There's a massive search going on in Hell's Porch. But all civilians have been ordered out because of the shooting."

She repeated the words to Akeem, who reached for the phone.

"The search isn't as massive as they make it appear. I think the cops might be involved somehow."

She couldn't hear what his brother responded to that.

"Okay," Akeem said, then held the phone out. "He wants you back."

But before she could find out what Flint wanted, a shot rang out in the night, ripping the phone from her hand. And in case she was wondering if the bullet had been meant for her or the phone, the next shot grazed her shoulder.

Pain seared across her skin, shock immobilizing her for a second before she crouched to make a smaller target. She was hit. She couldn't be hit. Christopher was in there somewhere, waiting for her to come for him. How could she have been this stupid? Instinct pushed her forward, toward her son.

Then Akeem was there, on top of her, dragging her to safety.

"YOU STUPID IDIOT!" Jake Kenner knocked the hired gun, Gabe, away from the window. "We're not supposed to kill the woman." The boss had been very specific about that.

Hate burned in Gabe's eyes as he turned back. He didn't like to be told what to do, that one. Which was why he hadn't been able to hold down a job for more than six months ever in his life. He cursed every ranch he ever worked, annoying the rest of the men to death. There was plenty of tension to go around without anyone bitching and moaning from dawn to dusk.

"She ain't supposed to be here." Gabe shrugged.

He had a point there. "Go upstairs and look around. See if there are cops with her. Don't shoot at anyone." He shoved the man off then looked through the window. Taylor McKade was gone and so was the man who'd been at her side a moment ago.

Damn.

He thought for a moment, then decided this constituted a major development. One the boss wasn't going to like, but the man would be angrier still if he found out that Jake had kept the news from him. He flipped his cell phone open and dialed.

"The McKade woman is here with her guy."

Silence stretched on the other end.

"Just the two of them?"

"Yes, sir." At first, he'd just wanted his cut of the money and everything to go as planned without anyone getting hurt. But little had gone the way they'd planned. Now he just wanted the whole damn thing to be over. He no longer cared who he'd have to hurt to get out of here with the money in his pockets.

"Keep them busy until morning," the voice said, then all he heard was a dial tone.

Jake closed his phone and pushed it back into his pocket. The boss made little sense. As long as they were here, why not take the money from them? Easy enough to have all three of them disappear in one of the tar pits, disappear forever should said tar pit catch fire by accident.

Odd that the boss hadn't asked about the money at all.

Jake had thought plenty about it during the past two days. And it ticked him off that the McKade woman and her lackey didn't seem to have anything with them.

He hadn't mentioned the phone to the boss. He would have only been yelled at for not shooting it before they'd had a chance to make the call. Or chewed him out for having allowed a shot at Taylor McKade in the first place. She wasn't to be hurt.

He'd been told that with some emphasis. The guy, though, could die, should die, before he had a chance to interfere. Whatever happened to the kid, happened. Maybe the boss had other plans for the woman. She was pretty enough, although not Jake's type. He preferred a saucy, easy-to-tumble barmaid any day of the week. Not that he could look that way these days. His new girlfriend was nothing if not territorial, with that gleam of marriage in her eyes. Still, she was a decent woman. He would have enough money soon. Maybe he would give marriage a try.

Who the hell knew what the boss had in mind for Taylor McKade? Who the hell cared?

Either way, mentioning the phone would have brought trouble, and it didn't much matter anyway. Even if a call had gone off to the cops, the boss had the cops taken care of. Then messing up the exchange at the boulders had been a mistake, the boss had promised, a mistake that wasn't going to happen again.

He would like to know how these two had gotten the damn phone to work. It was supposed to have been fixed to receive calls but not call out. But they had gotten one call out. If not more. That wasn't supposed to happen.

Keep them busy till morning. He didn't expect that would be too hard. Those two weren't going anywhere, not as long as he had the kid. There were three of them inside, armed to the teeth, and the other two coming soon. Taylor McKade and her guy might not have any weapons—they hadn't used any at the botched handover attempt—but he wouldn't underestimate them right off the bat.

But they *had* spent an awful long time trekking through the desert without much to eat and drink, likely without sleep. And he didn't think they knew the refinery. Most likely they'd followed the tracks of one of the pickups here. He hadn't expected that. Taylor could not have done that on her own. When he'd made his plans, he hadn't known that some guy would be coming with her, too. It might take them until morning just to find what they were looking for. Which would be perfect.

By then the boss would arrive and he could deal with them.

All Jake had to do was keep a tight rein on the sorry excuse of a team the boss had assembled. The men were growing restless locked up in here. Pete had gone off to buy some smokes. Jake hoped the guy would be back soon. He hoped Pete heeded his warning and wouldn't bring any booze back with him. Whiskey was the last thing Gabe and those other idiots needed.

He wished, not for the first time, that he could have pulled off the job on his own, but the boss had insisted on a whole team of hired help.

A bunch of incompetents. He would have to keep on his toes to make sure they didn't bring him down with them in the end.

Chapter Seven

Akeem shoved Taylor behind him. They needed to get out of the line of fire and to higher ground so that he could keep an eye on the movements of the enemy and figure out the layout of the buildings. There was enough moonlight for decent visibility, except in the deep shadows made by the taller buildings.

The solution presented itself as they rounded a towering storage tank. A rusty metal ladder ran up the side, all the way to the top. He helped her up in front of him, watched the dark stain spread on her shoulder. She'd been shot. Hurt again.

His jaw was clenched tight enough to snap. He eased the pressure so he could ask, "How bad is it?"

She halted for a second and reached for her arm. "Sticky." Then resumed climbing.

"A little or a lot?" Pain sliced into his thigh with every step as he climbed. He checked his own bandage, glad to see that the bleeding hadn't increased too badly, even with activity.

"Feels like a lot."

Anger and concern held him in a tight grip. He should have come alone. He should have somehow found a way—no matter what the kidnappers had said—to talk her out of coming with him.

He pushed her to go faster. They needed to

get up on top before they were discovered and someone opened fire on them.

Then Taylor reached the top and hesitated for a moment. He could see why. The actual roof was five feet below them on the other side. She straddled the ring that ran all around the edge of the roof, probably to protect it from heavy winds, which seemed to have damaged the roof anyway. He could make out several foot-wide holes. Luckily, they didn't have to get on the roof. There was a two-foot ledge inside of the protective ring, four feet down, probably used by maintenance at one time. She swung her feet over and dropped to crouch on the ledge, Akeem right on her heels.

"Stay right there."

She didn't look as if she was keen on exploring anyway. She was holding her arm.

He would get to that. He eased up first and looked out. No movement on the ground, no movement inside any of the buildings that he could see from here, no lights on anywhere. Maybe they would be okay for a few minutes.

He laid out the emergency supplies he'd gotten from the first-aid kit before leaving their bags behind: an alcohol wipe and a couple of large bandages. He'd planned on using them on Taylor's neck, but her arm needed them more. "Let's try to take off your shirt. Let me know if it hurts." He reached for her, awareness creeping into the moment immediately.

"It's not that bad." But she winced when he moved her arm.

He felt the cloth around the wound first, and after a while, breathed a little more easily. He didn't find as much blood as he had feared he would. But the wound was still bleeding. The forced pace of their climb probably hadn't helped.

"Stay still as much as you can." He unbuttoned her shirt and peeled it off her good arm first, so he would only need to move her injured arm as little as possible.

Since the wound was still fresh, at least they didn't have to worry about the material being stuck in dried blood, causing her further pain.

"Here."

The sleeve slipped off easily. Her T-shirt was in the way, too, the wound just above the shoulder. He wanted to see all of it, as much as he *could* see in the darkness. He tried to push the material aside, but it wasn't enough. So she reached for the hem and pulled the T-shirt over her head with her good hand. Which left her wearing precious little.

Don't look at the pale yellow lace. Not an

easy thing to do since it about glowed in the moonlight, definitely drawing attention.

Don't think of the feel of her skin.

Who was he kidding?

"So what's the verdict? Am I going to bleed to death?" She was saying the words jokingly, but he could hear the underlying worry in her voice and knew she wasn't as worried about herself as about her inability to help her son if something happened to her.

And here he was, lusting for her.

On some level, he knew he probably should be ashamed of himself, but damned if he could find that place. So since he couldn't not want her—even now, even here, always— he went for the next best thing, ignoring that he did.

"You'll be fine. I'm sure you've gotten into worse scrapes at the ranch."

"You don't know the half of it." Relief lightened her voice.

And he didn't want to. He hated to think of Taylor in any kind of danger or hurt.

He ripped the wrapper off the alcohol wipe. "This is going to sting."

Her indrawn hiss of air was the only response.

He made as quick a work of disinfecting the wound as he could, making sure he got all of it. The bullet hadn't gone in, just grazed her shoulder. But it did take a chunk of skin with it.

When he was done, working by nothing but moonlight, he positioned the bandages so they would cover the worst of the wound. He'd saved a corner of a wipe to clean the cut on her throat, his mood darkening by the minute. When he was done with that, he helped her get her shirt back on. They had no backup clothing here. As bloody and torn as the sleeve was, there was no help for that.

Only when he finally moved and the moonlight fell on her face did he see how her lips were pressed together, the tight set of her jaw.

Dammit. She wasn't hurt badly, but she shouldn't have gotten hurt at all.

"Still burning?"

"Like hell on high octane." She offered a pained smile.

He wished he could take her pain. He wanted to pull her into his arms, run his fingers down her hair and soothe her. But she wasn't likely to go for that. She wanted him gone. He winced at the memory of how he had kissed her in response.

"Look, I'm sorry about… Kissing you back there was… And that guy in the guardhouse. I had no choice, Taylor. I don't want you to think that you can't trust me. I know I'm not what you need, probably the last thing you need, but you have to let me—"

"I didn't mind the kiss."

He was so focused on how to word what he meant to say, that she'd confused him for a second. "What?"

"I don't mind it when you kiss me."

He stared at her. At her mouth, specifically. If only they had the time.

Another moment passed before other thoughts caught up with him again. "About the guy. I know what I did appeared savage. Hell, I was—"

"Thank you for saving my life."

Did she not mind what he'd done? But then why the *get away from me* speech? God, women were hard to understand at times, which hadn't bothered him all that much in the past. But he wanted to understand Taylor. "Why do you want to send me away?"

She didn't look like she was keen on giving him an answer. Looked on the exasperated side more than anything.

"Come on, Taylor."

For a moment she flattened her lips together. Something shifted in her eyes. "You have nothing to do with this."

He expelled the pent-up air in his lungs. "Everything that has to do with you, has to do with me," he said quietly. It was as good as a confession, but he had to make her understand.

"You're hurt," she said.

"So are you."

"You're hurt worse."

The corner of his mouth twitched up. "Is this a contest?"

"This might get—" She stopped as if to search for the right word. "If things go badly here…I don't want anything to happen to you."

His heart went wild banging in his chest. "Because?" he asked quietly.

"Because I care about you." She looked away. "So there."

Digesting that took a while. She cared about him. That was good. Great, in fact. He could build on that.

"Nothing's going to happen to me. Or to you. Or to Christopher. I swear," he said and reached out to put his fingers under her chin, turned her head, then bent his head to fit his lips to hers.

SHE COULD GET USED TO THIS. Kissing Akeem. Taylor settled against him, burrowing against his solid chest. His lips were warm on hers, gentle. Which was what she needed. The pain in her shoulder disappeared. He turned the kiss into something more urgent and demanding. Which was what she wanted.

He tasted her as if he never wanted to stop. And at this moment that was fine with her. There was such comfort in his touch.

Oblivion.

She gave herself over to the pleasure, her emotions exhausted from the day's events. She wanted the energy that vibrated through him and into her as he explored her.

How easy this was, she thought, and wondered if it would have been like this before, if he'd taken her seriously back then, if she hadn't run off when he'd seemed reluctant.

She didn't wonder long. What he was doing to her felt too good to spend mental energy second-guessing the past.

They pulled apart reluctantly. He rested his forehead against hers for a moment.

"Are you okay?" He searched her eyes in the moonlit night.

She hoped he couldn't see the heat in her face. The wound was fine, nothing but a dull throb that felt tight when she moved. Her head, however, was seriously spinning from his kisses.

She simply nodded. "What do we do next?"

Then caught herself and prayed he didn't think she meant what might follow kissing. Nothing was going to happen along those lines. They weren't on a date. High time she remembered that.

But he understood her without explanations and rose to look over the edge. "They're down there." He sat back down after a moment. "We wait until they give up searching, then we go down and find a back way into the building from where they shot at you. I bet that's where they're keeping Christopher."

She peeked out, and after minutes of straining her eyes could finally see one shadow that was deeper than the others. It might have moved a fraction of an inch.

She pulled back down. "So we're stuck here?"

"If we try to climb down now, they can pick us off easy as anything."

"Remind me again why we came up here?"

"We needed a place to hide. And I wanted to get a better idea of the layout of the refinery. At least now we know the exact relation of the buildings to each other. We can make a plan."

That made some sense. "But we could be stuck up here for hours."

He nodded.

"I'm going to go crazy." She stretched her legs, her arms, her back.

Silence settled between them as he watched.

Minutes passed before he spoke. "Why did you run off with Gary and marry him?"

SHE LOOKED AWAY, and for a moment Akeem didn't think she would answer, didn't know why he'd asked the stupid question in the first place. The night was filled with awareness between them and the last thing he wanted was to discuss Gary with her. And yet, part of him needed to know.

"He wanted me," she said after a while. "He did anything to get me. I was just so dazzled that he wanted me that badly. You have no idea how nice that felt." She shook her head.

The words *You had pushed me away,*

You didn't want me, hovered in the air between them.

"I was an idiot."

That earned him a smile. Which elicited another confession.

"However much Gary wanted you, I wanted you a hundred times worse."

Her eyes went wide. "You did?"

"I've been kicking myself since for not going after you when you ran off. Somebody should have."

"Why didn't you?"

"I was nobody. I had nothing to offer. And I figured Flint would kill me if he ever found out that I lusted after his baby sister."

She flashed a rueful smile. "I was hardly a baby. Flint did come after me, you know."

He shook his head. He hadn't known. Flint had never said anything about that.

"I didn't come back with him."

Would she have come back with Akeem? was the question that hung in the air between them.

"I'd been naïve and idealistic. Things were off with Gary from pretty early on. But I was too determined to make it work." She drew a deep breath. "I had to learn that not every mistake can be fixed. Some mistakes you just have to walk away from."

He watched her in the moonlight.

"You probably don't know much about mistakes." She gave a self-deprecating smile. "You've never put a foot wrong."

He gave a strangled laugh. "You'd be surprised."

"Look at the business you've built. You are a success. What am I?"

"A beautiful woman, inside and out, who learned her lessons from life. Someone who had the courage to walk away and start anew. A great mother. The beginning of a spectacular success story."

She looked surprised.

"The woman I still want," he added, and found that her eyes could go wider yet.

She didn't seem like she was used to compliments, so he decided to back up his words with action. He kissed her brows, her eyelids, kissed his way down the bridge of her nose, dragging out time before he brushed his lips over hers.

She was a woman to be savored.

She wasn't hurt badly. He thanked heaven for that. He'd be able to protect her. Another thing in their favor. For the moment, he refused to think of the million other things that stacked the odds against them.

For the moment, he allowed himself to taste

the sweetness of her lips, to run his fingers through the silk of her hair. The moon and the stars shined above them. And it was all slow and easy and good for a while. Then an urgency crept between them again, just like it had at the guardhouse.

Things could not get as out of hand again as they had back there, he thought in the last coherent corner of his brain. Then reassured himself that they *had* been able to stop in time. They would stop again.

So he allowed his hands to caress her face, her uninjured arm, her breasts. And when she moaned into his mouth, he swallowed the sound.

She reached for his shirt to pull it up. He let her. Then held his breath as her slim fingers explored his abdomen and moved up to his chest. She set his body buzzing with need. A need he would ignore. All he would do was distract her for a while, relax her.

He, himself, was feeling far from relaxed.

Every muscle in his body was drawn hard, focused on the pleasure of her touch, the pleasure that came from him touching her. When she tugged off his shirt all the way, he didn't protest.

The night breeze glided along his back, cool. Taylor in his arms, hot as fire. He was more than willing to let himself burn up in her flame.

He brushed aside her shirt and wanted badly to take her T-shirt off, but didn't want to hurt her arm—he no longer felt his own pain. Her T-shirt would stay. A good limit to set to ensure that things didn't get out of hand between them.

But he did want another look at that pale yellow bra, so he pushed the T-shirt up. He kissed the underside of her breasts, then found his way to the lace cups. She arched her back when he flicked his tongue against a hardened nipple.

Then he got carried away just a little.

When she made a sound like a woman who desperately needed release, it seemed like the logical thing to unzip her pants and slide his hand inside. His fingers combed through her silky curls, dipped into her moist heat.

She was going for his pants. Absolutely nothing was going to happen, but he had no heart to stop her. He let her do as she wished. And that was when things got dangerous. Because the frantic seconds that followed left him in his underwear. And her pants were tangled up in the pile with his, along with two guns and their knife.

Oh, man.

It only *looked* like something was going to happen, because it wasn't. Going to. At all.

He started to backpedal to that end. Removing himself from on top of her seemed like a good first step. So he pulled back and sat on the ledge, his back to the outer wall, trying to catch his breath. And congratulated himself for having kept a cool head.

They would catch their breath, suffer some awkward silence, then it would be as if this had never happened. Which really was the best outcome at this particular moment in time, although definitely not the one every cell in his body was begging for.

Nothing.

Was.

Going.

To.

Happen.

But then she came and straddled him. His hands might have gone to her hips to help her off, but they ended up holding on to make sure she stayed in place. And even as she lowered herself, his body rose on its own. And then he was pressing against her.

Heat.

Friction.

Desire.

They still had some clothes on. Very little, but at least it was something. As long as they had that, they couldn't get carried away, could they? He put his hands on her under-wear to make sure it stayed in place. That worked for about three seconds before his fingers slipped under yellow lace, dipped toward the center from where all the heat seemed to be radiating. She arched her back, and made a low sound in her throat, pressed harder against him. Pleasure spread through him in response, as they rocked against each other. An eternity passed with them lost in each other's bodies. Old desires heated to a fever pitch, old fantasies coming true at last.

He buried his face between her breasts and pulled her tighter to him if that was possible. Control was slipping out of his hands. His body sought hers mindlessly. Everywhere they touched, pleasure seemed to seep into him through his very skin. *Slow,* he bade himself. And then moved faster.

Slim fingers teased the elastic band around his waist.

He held his breath.

Her fingers sneaked inside.

A tremor ran through his muscles. Control was what he needed.

Good luck with that.

"Taylor. I'm too—" His voice was so deep and raspy he barely recognized it. And as her fingers closed around him, he couldn't finish the warning.

Breathe.

Sure, if only that were possible.

They held each other's gazes as release claimed them at last, and he wished the moon was brighter so he could see her face more clearly.

Then she collapsed into his arms, and he held her, spent in passion, wondering if this was the right time to tell her that he was never going to let her go again.

They were pressed together so tightly, as if fused at the core. Her heart beat wildly against his.

And she still had her T-shirt on.

She lifted her head after a few minutes and

looked at him with a dazzled look about her. "What happened?"

"Fate," he said, and savored the feel of her body entwined with his own, wanting to soak in every second of the reprieve he had a feeling might be very short-lived.

Chapter Eight

"Anything?" Taylor asked once Akeem had pulled back from surveying the area below. She was ignoring the fact that her body still hummed with pleasure. She hadn't said two words to him since they had dressed.

And putting clothes on had been quite the trick up on top of a storage tower, in the dark, on a two-foot-wide ledge. How they'd manage to… What had happened *before* the getting-dressed part was another question. Which she

was not going to think about. And was definitely not going to talk about with him.

"Don't do this," he said.

"See that cloud of guilt?" She pointed
above her head. "It can't be too easy to miss
since it's darker than Hell's Porch at midnight
and twice as large."

"Don't do this to yourself."

She couldn't address what had happened
between them. Absolutely not. Not now,
and possibly not ever. "What did you see
down there?"

He kept his gaze on her face as if hoping for
something else, then let it go after a moment.
"They're still watching. Still in hiding."

Which meant he couldn't do a thing to
disable them, so she was stuck on the roof
with him. Climbing down with the enemy
waiting in their secure positions would have

equaled suicide. Still, she couldn't help the guilt that ate at her for forgetting about her mission even for a short while, for giving in to her own need for comfort. She was a mother. She should have no needs. Should not be scared. Should not be exhausted.

"So your grandfather didn't like this place?" Akeem was examining their hideout on the inside now. "Can't blame him."

Something teased the edge of her memory, danced out of grasp before she could snatch it. "He didn't like the way they treated their employees. Saved a lot of money on safety." She'd been pretty young back then, didn't remember much of those conversations among adults.

Her grandfather had been blue collar all the way. Short stints at various refineries, working as a day laborer on the megafarms of the area in between. A decent man if dirt-poor. Akeem's grandfather had been a sheik. Royalty. According to Flint, he had oil pumps in Beharrain.

But to Akeem's credit, never once had he let their differences be felt between them. He had, in fact, chosen to make his own fortune instead of taking his share of his grandfather's billions. She had a feeling there was something other than money he might have wanted from the old man, but never gotten. At least her grandfather had loved her. That was more precious to her than any financial heritage. Her mother had been a cook—and part-time quilter—and her father a poor ranch hand, but she was proud of them both.

One particular summer night behind the barn floated into her mind, talking about old times by a fire, the whole family lounging around. And she remembered now the story of her grandfather's best friend's accident, and the rescue that had come too late for the man. And then it all clicked.

"I know! There's a ladder somewhere on the inside, too. There's a maintenance door near the bottom."

He took her face in his hands and kissed her soundly on the mouth, but she pulled back, then looked away from his searching gaze. An awkward moment passed between them. Then they were moving along the ledge.

"You could stay here until I find a way down," he said.

She couldn't have stayed still for all the treasure in the world. She needed to be moving, doing something, anything, that took her closer to Christopher. "I'm going with you."

To his credit, he didn't argue. He simply said, "Be careful where you step."

He was right to be cautious. Judging by the condition of the rest of the structure, stepping on a weak spot and falling straight through was a real possibility.

"What did they keep in these things?" he asked. "Crude oil?"

"No idea." She followed close behind so she could grab him if he slipped. "All Gramps ever talked about was tar."

They moved ahead in silence, their full attention on their next step.

"How is your shoulder?" he asked after a while.

All but forgotten. "Okay. How is your leg?"

"Ready for the Texas two-step, anytime you are." His response was light, but she could see his limp in the moonlight.

Even if the bandage was tight enough to prevent serious blood loss, infection was a distinct possibility. For the both of them. They needed to grab Christopher then get out of here.

"Here we go," he said as he stopped.

And she could see the open metal trapdoor and the top of a ladder careful not to make too much noise. The smell of gasoline was much stronger here. The space was pitch-dark below them, no telling what they were getting into.

"What if there's oil or tar or something nasty down there?" Her idea of reaching the ground this way seemed risky and foolish all of a sudden.

"I doubt they'd leave anything valuable behind. But if we hit something sticky, we'll climb back up. We won't be any worse off than we are now."

That made sense. She watched him reach

down and shake the ladder. It held. "Might work." He swung his good leg over first, wouldn't let go of the opening until he tested that the ladder would hold his weight.

She moved closer.

"Wait until I give some kind of signal," he said. "I'd rather we went one at a time."

Which made sense, but she hated staying on the roof all alone. Still, they had no way of assessing how much the rusty ladder could handle. So she nodded and stayed where she was.

The next half hour was nerve-racking. She sat close to the trapdoor, peering into the darkness below without seeing anything, listening for the slightest noise from below.

She didn't dare shout down to check on him for fear that she would give away what they were doing. And she didn't dare go after him until he gave a signal, but no signal was coming.

Then, when she was squirming in desperation, and contemplating what she would have to do if he got hurt somehow and there would be no signal coming at all, a gentle tap reverberated up the metal ladder. She offered a quick prayer toward the starlit sky before she grabbed the top of the ladder and climbed after Akeem.

Going over the edge and putting her feet on the top rung was even scarier than she had expected, her step unsure all of a sudden. She could see nothing below. There could be anything down there. She could grab onto a poisonous spider on any of the rungs, or get knocked off by a swarm of bats.

She moved fast, eager to be done with this part and be closer to Akeem, ignoring the pain when the skin pulled around the bullet graze on her shoulder. She didn't care much about her existing injuries at this point. She was focused on not acquiring any new ones. She was halfway down when something banged above her, and her only source of light was suddenly shut off.

Somebody had climbed up after them, figured out where they had gone, and had shut the trapdoor.

The enemy knew where they were, and they were trapped once again. And whether there were any combustible materials left over down below or not, she had a feeling that the fumes alone in this place were enough to send it exploding all over creation if someone tossed as much as a single match their way.

She was frozen to the spot where she'd

stopped, her fingers fused to the ladder as she gasped for air in the dark. Tense moments passed as she hung on for dear life with white-knuckled hands.

A few seconds passed.

Then a soft whisper came from not too far below. "It's okay, Taylor. I'm waiting for you down here."

And she hung on to that voice, trusting it to lead her. She made her limbs obey her once again. An eternity seemed to pass before she made it down all the way and found herself in Akeem's arms.

"This way." He pulled her forward.

His night vision must have been much better than hers, as she could barely see his back, but he apparently could tell where they were going since he kept a good pace. She had no choice but to trust herself completely to him, believe his promises at last that he would help her get her son back.

"Do you think they're waiting for us somewhere ahead?" she whispered.

"I'm sure there is more than one door on this tower."

A small noise came from the far side of the structure. They stopped to listen, but couldn't hear anything more.

"Could be just a possum or whatever other animal nests in here." Akeem resumed walking, drawing her with him, not letting her hand go for a moment.

"Why aren't they doing more to find us?" They'd taken their sweet time coming after them.

"They probably know who we are and what we want. They know we'll be coming to them."

"Then why come after us at all?"

"Could be one of them got antsy waiting. Wanted to play around a little."

"So you definitely think they're waiting for us now?"

"Yes."

She drew a deep breath from the dank, fume-filled air. "Do you think there are only two of them? There were only two pickups at that loading dock. And when we last saw them, there was only one guy in each."

"Doesn't mean they didn't have more here in reserve. It's always best to be prepared for the worst."

He sounded calm and collected, reasonable. A far cry from her own state of mind. "How bad do you think it's going to get?"

Again, she felt a pang of regret that she had dragged him into this, and profound relief that he was here with her.

He stopped and she bumped against his wide back. "What is it?"

"The door."

"They could be waiting behind it."

"We'll know in a minute." He nudged her to the side. The knob scraped as he turned it.

Fresh air hit her in the face, a sliver of moonlight falling in. He moved forward. She held her breath.

"All clear," he said.

They moved outside with caution, but it seemed that if the men were waiting for them, they waited at another exit. Akeem said nothing, but pulled a serious-looking handgun from the back of his waistband— the weapon they had found in the dead guy's pickup—and handed it to her.

She took it and checked it. She had half a magazine's worth of bullets. She had no trouble with guns. When she rode out to the farthest corners of the ranch, she always carried one for protection from the wildlife.

She was painfully aware that when she fired this piece, she would be shooting at people, and that was a new, disturbing thought.

She turned the gun over in her hand, and thought of the guy Akeem had killed. For her. For Christopher. The full impact hadn't hit her until now when she had a weapon in her own hands and was preparing to use it if necessary. Akeem had killed for her and was willing to die for her. To save her son. There was no way in the universe she would ever be able to come close to repaying him for all he was doing.

He wasn't a callous man. What he had done would cost him. She had always thought of him as a gentleman, a consummate businessman, with a sharp mind and a lot of kindness behind those dark eyes. She'd caught glimpses of fire, too, now and then, fire that, for the most, he kept carefully hidden.

But he was a warrior, too.

A warrior on her side.

"I know I said you should go back—"

"Taylor. Not now. Let's give that a rest." The tone of his voice indicated that this particular topic was beginning to try his patience.

"I'm trying to say that I'm really, really happy that you're here."

He was silent for a moment. "As I said, I'm not going anywhere without you and Christopher," he said, then stopped to stare at a stocky building with a tall, round brick chimney towering over it.

If *chimney* was the right word. The thing was more like a skinny tower, situated on the ground next to the building and reaching toward the sky, tapering toward the top.

They could hear voices coming from behind the storage tower they had just left. Two men at least, probably looking for them.

"I think they're going in the other direction. For now," Akeem said.

Oh, no. She had a bad feeling about this. "We are climbing again, aren't we?"

"From the ground, there is only one way into the building," he said. "I really think he is here."

And she had to agree. That was where the pickups were parked.

"So it's a given that the entrance would be guarded. We can't go in through there," he went on.

She really hated what was coming.

"But the chimney runs all the way up the

side of the building, and there's a short con-necting bridge up there." He pointed up.

He did have super vision, she thought after a moment, when after considerable effort she finally made out the dim lines of something that might have been the bridge he was talking about.

"How is your arm?" he asked again.

"Fine." As long as she didn't think about it. Which wasn't hard. Compared to the fact that they could be shot at any minute, compared to her worries about Christopher, the dull throb in her arm barely merited attention.

The corners of his eyes crinkled. "You're pretty tough, for a girl."

He'd used to tell her that back in the day all the time. Of course, she'd had a tendency to show off for him back then.

"Did I have to grow up with Flint or what?

Self-preservation *was* the name of the game."

The corner of his mouth twitched. "I bet."

They stood there for a long moment before she realized why they had stopped moving. To reach the chimney they were headed for, they would have to walk out into the open, no other way to get there. He was probably worried. About her. But she couldn't let that stop him. They were here for Christopher. She was willing to risk any amount of bodily injury to get him back.

So she stepped out of the shadows first and kept low as she ran toward the side of the building opposite them, her gun ready. There were no windows on this side, but the walls were made of corrugated steel in places and had plenty of holes. If anyone was looking, they'd definitely be seen.

She held her breath until she reached the wall, flattened against it just as Akeem caught up with her a second later.

"Maybe they didn't see us." She caught her breath that was labored not from the effort, but from sheer nerves.

"Maybe they're busy setting a trap."

"You want to scare me?" They'd made it through the open; he could have been more positive just for a second.

"I want you to think before you act." His voice had some bite to it. "Or, at least, give some warning before you leap."

Okay. Fine. He was right. She was about to say so, but he was already heading toward the chimney that had a row of frighteningly rusty metal spikes going up the side.

No guardrail.

Clouds drifted across the moon, dimming

visibility further yet, but as she stepped to the towering chimneystack, she could make out now that it was a lot bigger around than she'd judged from afar. Over twelve feet in diameter at the base, if not more. Not as flimsy as it had looked. Thank God for that.

He tested the first spike, stepped on it, reached as far as he could, tested that spike before putting his weight on it, then placed his foot on the next. "Try to put your feet where I do," he said.

No problem there. She had plenty of motivation to pay attention.

"And stay a little back," he warned.

He meant in case he slipped, she realized after a moment and was glad he thought of everything. She was too frazzled to think beyond the next step, her mind on Christopher.

She would not allow herself to think that her little boy might not be here.

The climb was nerve-racking, and she prayed all the way. They were nearly level with the roof when a shout sounded somewhere inside the building. The first bullet wasn't far behind.

No time to finagle their way onto the narrow brick bridge that served not as a walkway but as a link to secure the chimney to the building and give it extra stability. Akeem lunged, caught the edge of the flat roof, swung his legs and pulled himself up, then reached for her. She had to let go and catapult herself over the five-foot gap that stood between the chimney and the building.

For a moment, she had nothing beneath her but air and a hundred-foot drop to a cement slab below. The she felt Akeem's hand close around hers.

Shc had just enough time to catch her breath before she realized that she was slipping.

She grabbed with her other hand and caught his sleeve, heard and felt the fabric rip. Another bullet slammed into the old bricks close enough to send dust into her eyes.

She blinked, trying to clear the tears that gathered to wash out the dust particles, as she dangled over the abyss, held by nothing but a torn sleeve and hcr fingertips.

Boots pounded on metal stairs somewhere below them, inside the building.

"Try to swing back to the chimney." Akeem helpcd by giving hcr a boost.

She let go of his half-torn sleeve that wouldn't have supported her anyway, shoved her feet against the side of the building. Her other hand did slip out of Akeem's then, and she did fall.

But she fell in the right direction, and she could lurch her weight toward the spikes. She grabbed on to one, and just barely avoided another one skewering her side.

"Go around." Akeem jumped to a spike above her with his usual graceful agility.

"Around where?" She looked around, bewildered.

There was shouting on the roof now. Those men would reach the edge in seconds and pick her and Akeem off with two easy shots.

But Akeem was already moving, and she could see now that a lot of the bricks had been damaged over the years, chunks missing here and there. He was moving foothold by foothold, handhold by handhold to put the chimneystack between him and the approaching men.

She didn't hesitate, but did the same.

The chimney was wide enough even up here, so that if they made it to the other side, they would be completely invisible from the roof.

She barely slipped out of view when she heard, "Where the hell are they?" bellowed with full force.

Some shuffling sounded next.

"Could be they climbed down and got in on the floor below us," another voice responded.

There was a moment of silence, then, "Jimmy stays here."

The sound of boots on the roof came next, running in the opposite direction.

She looked at Akeem.

He mouthed a single word, "Stay."

She didn't have a problem with that. She watched with her heart in her throat as he inched to the side. Peeked around. Pulled back.

Then he let go with his right hand. And she

was shaking with nerves just watching him. Their situation was precarious enough. All her strength was barely enough to keep her where she was. If one foot or hand slipped, she would fall to her death. And here he was, willfully dangling.

She held her breath as he pulled a knife, leaned to the side again, then aimed. The weapon sailed through the air with a hiss, closely followed by a thud.

Then Akeem was moving forward. "I got him. Come on."

She didn't hesitate. The iron spikes that had seemed way too flimsy before now felt like the height of security. Akeem pulled himself up to the bridge and reached back for her. This time, they made it to the roof without trouble.

Akeem took the guy's gun and stuck it into

his waistband next to his other weapon. He didn't bother with the knife.

She hesitated for a second, bent over, pulled it from the man's chest then wiped the blade and put it away. She only shrugged at Akeem's questioning look. It wasn't just the tough-for-a-girl thing anymore. She was being tough for her son.

They stole across the roof, down the stairs and found themselves on a gangplank inside that overlooked some odd machinery. Nobody down there that she could see. Maybe the men had already moved on with their search. Everything smelled oily, even in here.

Akeem crept across the gangplank, then down to the floor below. She followed just as carefully. A long wall divided the space, closing off the area to their left. They moved along the wall, in the cover of some pipes.

When they came across a window opening to another space, they dipped low and walked in a crouch, and since she was shorter than Akeem, she caught a gap in the wall that Akeem hadn't. Something moved on the other side.

Akeem wasn't looking at her, and she couldn't say anything. Anyone on the other side could hear.

The board next to the gap was loose. She moved it a fraction at a time, stopped as soon as she had an inch or so to look through, although she could have moved it farther.

Christopher was sleeping in a corner not ten feet from her. Tears gathered in her eyes at the sight of his sweet, smudged little face. She blinked them away to clear her vision. She'd cry later, tears of joy, when her son was back in her arms again.

Her heart lurched into a mad race. He was here. God, they were so close. She pulled back to survey the board. Akeem was way ahead of her now. Something was drawing his attention there, and he hadn't noticed that she had stayed behind.

And she still didn't dare make a sound. So she turned her attention to something she could do—the board.

The gap was too small for her to get in. But if she could somehow get her son's attention, he could come to her. She could possibly move that board enough for him to squeeze through.

Maybe whoever was guarding him was sleeping, too, or had left the room to search the building with the others for her and Akeem. Try as she might, she couldn't see the whole room from her vantage point.

Wake up, honey. Wake up and come to Mommy. She sent her thoughts across the space between them. Christopher did stir, but didn't open his eyes.

Probably wouldn't have made a difference if she said the words aloud. He always could sleep through anything from summer storms to tractor motors. He was just like her brother, Flint.

She had slid the board back as far as she could. She hadn't made a noise so far. The hole was big enough. He would fit, she knew he would. Please, God, let him be alone in there.

He was so close. He could make his way over to her in seconds. Once he was close enough to the hole, she could reach in and pull him through. Then she would grab him up and rush after Akeem. Akeem would find a way to lead them out of here.

Mommy is here. Everything is going to be fine. Wake up, baby.

Christopher shifted in his sleep again. Which was when she spotted the rope around his right ankle. He was tied to some pipe that ran along the wall behind his back. He was trapped.

Chapter Nine

Taylor hated, absolutely hated, letting her son out of her sight, but she had to get Akeem. So she pushed away and scurried after him, making as little noise as possible.

"He's here," she whispered when she caught up with him at the top of the stairway.

"You've seen him?" He mouthed the words as his gaze settled on her for a second before going back to scanning the area.

"Back there."

"Guards?"

"Can't tell. He's—" She swallowed. "Tied up." But he looked unharmed, and that infused her heart with new hope.

"Looking okay?"

She nodded, and tears threatened to spill again. Every atom of her body was pulling her back to that hole in the wall. "Sleeping."

"We'll get him. I swear," he said just as someone stepped into the stairway below them.

Boots pounded up the metal steps.

All she could think of was that they could not get caught this close to Christopher. It would be so incredibly unfair.

Akeem pulled her into the cover of a rusty column that only protected them from one side, and gently pressed his index finger against her lips. Then his body to hers. Close then closer, so that the two of them would take up as little space as possible.

AKEEM WAS AWARE OF many things at once: Taylor pressed tight against him, the tangled jumble of his feelings for her and the growing danger that surrounded them.

He felt that hard resolution rise up in him. He didn't like what was to come, but he would do it anyway.

The four years spent in the desert with his grandfather had brought him face-to-face with his warrior heritage and not all of it had been pleasant. Some parts had been downright shocking.

He had seen his grandfather kill. He would be hard-pressed to forget the two-hundred-year-old sword that had chopped off the head of a tribesman who'd been caught transporting drugs through tribal land. He also knew that his grandfather would have killed his mother if she hadn't escaped to the U.S. Would have considered it an honor killing and the righteous thing to do since the girl was found carrying a child before being wed.

He'd seen his grandfather cut off the hand of a thief, and order the caning of a young boy for some minor sin. He'd seen his grandfather in battle, bathed in the blood of his enemies.

In the same battle where Akeem had first killed at the age of sixteen. And had wondered how much of that ruthless wildness ran in his own blood. He had sworn never to shed his humanity on that level again, an oath he had broken already, and in front of Taylor.

He had wanted to be a better man than that for her. He wanted to be all that was good and civilized. But he would do whatever he needed to do to keep her and her son safe. He would kill again and again if he had to. He would die if he had to. He would make a deal with the very devil.

And he might have to do that soon. As in right now.

Someone was coming up the stairs.

Akeem shoved his gun into his waistband, positioned himself and waited until the guy passed him. When he lunged, he made sure that his right arm would go around the windpipe. A sharp, yanking move up and back would crush it. He didn't let up on the pressure, held tight as the man struggled, held while the guy kicked out, clawing Akeem's arm, held as those furiously kicking legs went slack.

He wouldn't look at Taylor as he held the man a few seconds longer to make sure that he was finished, then dragged him to the empty oil barrel under the turn of the stairs and dumped him inside, covered him with an oily rag he found on the floor.

"Show me where you saw Christopher," he said, still not looking at her, because he didn't want to see the revulsion that must sit plainly on her face.

She'd seen him kill three times within as many hours, commit the worst violence. And he had a suspicion that she had barely escaped from a rough and violent marriage. Would she think that he was exactly the kind of man she was escaping from? He hated the thought of that, yet couldn't be a hundred percent sure that she wouldn't be right thinking it of him, and worse. He wasn't sure if he could stand having her be afraid of him.

But she surprised him by stepping right up to him and moving into his arms, as if she weren't afraid of him at all, as if she were seeking shelter in his embrace. For a moment, he wasn't sure who was comforting whom. A couple of seconds passed before she moved away and visibly pulled herself together.

"This way," she whispered.

They backtracked the way they had come, and he followed her, gun at the ready, until she came to crouch by one of the holes low on the wall. He would have known from the look on her face what she was looking at on the other side, even if she hadn't already told him. The tenderness mixed with worry in her eyes was gut-wrenching.

He looked behind them one last time before he crouched next to her to assess the situation at hand.

Christopher slept like the four-year-old that he was, mouth hanging open, oblivious to the world. His face was smudged, his blond hair sticking up every which way. Akeem registered the rope on his ankle and the red mark that it had rubbed on his skin, and his jaw tightened.

From his vantage point, he couldn't tell if there were any other people in the room with the boy. Nor could he see an entry on the opposite wall. Maybe to the right? He twisted, and the back of his head came into contact with something cold and hard.

"I got them," a voice called out cheerfully behind him.

Then the guy whacked Akeem hard in the back of the skull.

SHE SHOULD HAVE KEPT watch while Akeem had looked. Fury at the men who held them raged in Taylor's blood, mixing with anger at her own stupidity. She hadn't been able to tear herself away from the sight of Christopher, had crouched with eyes glued to a gap in the boards.

But now all she could see was the blood on the back of Akeem's head. They were shoving him ahead, in front of her.

A metal door banged open. Akeem was kicked inside. They pushed her behind him. Into *the* room.

"Christopher!" She tore herself from the man who held her and lunged toward her little boy, folding to the floor next to him, frustrated that she couldn't hug him to herself with her hands tied behind her back.

But those little arms came around her neck as soon as his baby blue eyes opened. "Mommy?"

The men, three of them in the room, didn't seem to bother with her. They were all focused on Akeem. So she pulled back a little and greedily took stock of her son, examining every inch. "Are you okay?"

"I knew you would come." Christopher scrambled onto her lap. "Can we go home now? I don't like it here."

"We—"

The thud coming from behind her had her whipping her head around.

Akeem was halfway to the floor. She watched as the man in front of him delivered a vicious kick to his knee—another thud—and Akeem crashed to the ground. Instinct had her move protectively in front of Christopher to block the sight. She could do nothing at all to help Akeem.

"No, please don't," she pleaded with the men, but they paid no attention.

Another one kicked Akeem's back, sending

him face-first onto the floor. He looked stunned from the pistol-whipping he'd gotten when they had been captured. More kicks came as he struggled to get up, struggled to fight back, although he could do little being all tied up.

The two men were brutal. She flinched when she heard the crack of a rib. Christopher pressed closer to her back and whimpered.

"Jake, please." She addressed the only man she knew in the room.

But Jake Kenner stood back, letting the other two take care of the dirty work, holding a gun on Akeem in case he got the upper hand by some miracle.

Which would have been impossible.

He'd fought hard when they'd been captured, but could do little against guns, gave up when they put one to her head. That was when they'd first gone to town on him, beating him to within inches of losing consciousness.

And they seemed hell-bent on finishing what they had started. They didn't stop until he was a bleeding heap on the floor.

"Take him out into the desert and get rid of him," Jake said dispassionately, in a voice colder than she had ever heard from the man. From any man, even Gary on his worst day. "Make sure he's dead."

He watched as his buddies hooked a hand under Akeem's arms and dragged him across the floor, then he turned those cold eyes on Taylor.

"And now, you are going to tell me where the money is."

She curled around her son as much as possible, not knowing if the words she was about to say were enough to save Akeem, or if they would be a death sentence for her and Christopher.

"I don't know. Only Akeem does. He hid it."

The men dragging him paused and turned, and a silent communication passed between them and Jake before they moved on.

Jake waited until they were gone before he pushed away from the table he'd been leaning against. "Either you're telling the truth, or you aren't. One way to find out." He flashed a slow smile as he pulled a knife she recognized. The standard utility knife Flint supplied all his ranch hands with. "And we have plenty of time to do it."

His body was moving toward unconsciousness to escape the pain, but Akeem was fighting it. He needed to pay attention to where they were taking him so he could find his way back to Taylor. He needed to figure out a way to escape summary execution. He wasn't sure how much time Taylor and Christopher had left.

One of the men who'd dragged him out was in the cab, driving, the other was sitting in the back of the pickup with Akeem.

"She was telling the truth," he said, just loudly enough so the guy next to him could hear as they bounced over uneven ground in the night.

The driver followed no road. Probably so Akeem's body wouldn't readily be found.

"I wouldn't let her see where I buried the money so if she got caught, she couldn't tell. She's a woman." He made a dismissive sound. "She wouldn't stand up to questioning."

If these two thought he had something, they might give him a little more time. He needed a minute or two to focus away from the pain and make his broken body obey his will once again. He was little more than a heap of bruised flesh at the moment.

The guy wouldn't look at him, but from the way his eyes were focused, he appeared to be listening.

"This is going to go down badly. You know that. Whatever the original plan was, it's gone way off track. Her brother is a powerful man," Akeem went on.

The guy simply shrugged.

"How much is your cut? Can't be too much. Too many people are involved. There were expenses. Someone had to pay off the police."

He was fishing around in the dark, but the guy didn't protest that last assumption. Anger boiled in Akeem's blood. So the cops *had* been paid off. That—and not safety concerns— was why no civilian aircraft were being allowed over Hell's Porch. They were making sure that no rescue was coming.

"I know where the money is. You help me get out of this, it's all yours. Just yours. For one man, it's enough to disappear and live a pretty fine life for the next seventy years or so."

The man looked at him at last. "What if you're lyin'?"

Akeem breathed a little easier. The shark was nibbling the hook. "You know I had the money yesterday. You saw me with the brief-cases. I still have it. I can show you where."

"And if it's a trick?"

"You'll still have your gun." He shrugged as if saying, *you could always shoot me then.*

The thug seemed to mull that over, but shook his head when he got to the end of his silent reasoning. "The boss would kill me dead."

"Jake will never find you. When I go back for the woman and the kid, I'll take care of him, I swear to that." The bastard could take that to the bank.

But the guy sneered. "Jake ain't nothin'."

Akeem paused to digest that. So there was another boss. Someone bigger and more powerful. Which made sense. Someone who had the police in his back pocket.

The whole thing was starting to sound eerily familiar. Like what had happened at the airstrip with that plane that had carried Flint's horses a couple of months back. They had a powerful enemy whose sole purpose seemed to be to bring them down. Why? And who was it? And how did kidnapping Christopher play into the bastard's plans?

If the man behind all this was as powerful as Akeem suspected, two million dollars wouldn't be worth the risk of getting involved in a federal crime.

Not that two million wasn't a respectable amount. He needed to convince his newfound friend of just that.

"Two million will buy you a hell of a lot of protection. The way I look at it, it's your best chance to stay alive. Because before all this is said and done, one of your buddies is going to figure he'd be happier if he didn't have to cut the paycheck quite so many ways. Then there is the chance the boss might decide to eliminate his liabilities. Big men like that, they don't like to leave witnesses. They have too much to lose."

And the bastard was going to lose everything, if Akeem had anything to do with it. "Think this over. It could be your last chance. Two million dollars—"

He was cut off when the pickup stopped in the middle of nowhere.

"Shut up." The man stood and opened the tailgate, took the safety off his gun then kicked Akeem to the ground.

Landing knocked the air out of Akeem's lungs. He stayed motionless while he waited for the pain in his ribs to abate. If he could get his hands loose, he might stand a chance, but they were tied good and proper, the way you would expect from a couple of ex-cowboys who had more than a passing acquaintance with ropes.

"Get the shovel," the blond guy who'd been driving said as he got out of the cab.

"What shovel?" the other one asked.

"You didn't bring the damn shovel?"

His buddy shrugged.

The scene was starting to look like some

screwball comedy, but Akeem was grateful for anything that would keep them occupied for now. He wiggled his hands behind his back, trying to stretch the rope enough to slip out of it. At this stage, leaving some skin behind was the least of his worries.

The blond guy swore. "How in hell are we supposed to get rid of him, dumbass?"

A moment of silence came, then, "The bushes?"

"Yeah, genius? And have the coyotes drag him all over creation by morning? Don't you think there'll be a search for him sooner or later?"

"So? He'll be dead."

The blond guy spit on the rocks at his feet. "No body, no crime." His hand twitched on his gun. "You want this to come back to you someday, stupid?"

The other guy seemed to consider this, then nodded toward the pickup. "Got a handsaw in the toolbox. But between the wild hogs, the coyotes and the buzzards, I don't think we got much to worry about."

Akeem yanked harder on the ropes.

"I'll get the saw. You take care of him." The driver set his gun down to jump up in the back.

The guy who'd been keeping Akeem company on the road pointed his gun at Akeem's head.

This was the end. He had seconds. If he didn't figure out how to escape, Taylor and Christopher would be defenseless in the bastards' hands.

"Two million. Best chance you'll ever have." Akeem positioned his legs to swipe the thug's legs from under him.

But in the end, that wasn't necessary. The

man turned and fired at the driver, point-blank. Clean shot, middle of the forehead. The body tumbled over the side and to the ground. He hadn't even had time to look surprised.

Then the gun was pointed at Akeem.

"You better know where that money is and it better be close," the man said, undisguised desperation sitting on his face. He'd made his choice and knew if this didn't pan out, he was a dead man.

"It's at the refinery." Akeem would have told the guy that even if it weren't the truth. He needed to get back there ASAP.

The man grabbed him by the rope that held his hands and dragged him up.

"Hang on," Akeem gasped. "I think my ribs are broken. Just give me a second here." It wouldn't hurt to appear weak, not that he had to fake the pain. He leaned against the back of the pickup, breathed hard while he swiped the dead guy's gun and tucked it behind his back. He took a couple of deep breaths. "I can't get back up here if you don't untie my hands."

The guy shoved him away to close the tailgate. "You're going in the cab." He nudged him forward and pushed him up.

Akeem lay back in the passenger seat, his head still pounding from the beating he'd gotten, his ribs sore from movement. He got dizzy every time he moved, probably from the original pistol-whipping. Even if by some miracle he managed to free himself, he was in no condition to drive. So he took the chance to rest and gather up his energy for the fight that was to come when they reached the refinery.

As the pickup started then turned to rattle over the rocky ground, he prayed that Taylor and Christopher were still alive.

Taylor had told Jake that Akeem had the money. Which had probably saved his life.

But this same grand gesture made her and her son disposable.

"COME ON, JAKE." TAYLOR wiped her split lip.

He had his knife in his left hand, but hadn't used it yet. And now she remembered someone saying back at the ranch that he didn't like blood, and she hoped he never would. That he was just trying to scare her.

"Flint did right by you. He gave you a job, food and a roof over your head. Don't do this."

"Where is the money?"

"Kidnapping is one thing. Murder will follow you everywhere. The world is getting smaller every day. The cops have databases in every country. They're all linked to each other. You can't run from capital crime in this day and age."

"Where is the money?"

"I don't know. Akeem had it." She braced for the next slap, keeping Christopher behind her, out of sight, out of Jake's mind.

That strategy had worked until now, but it seemed Jake was getting tired of his slap-and-ask game. He walked around her, grabbed the little boy by the arm and yanked him roughly to his feet.

"Maybe the kid needs to clear his head. What do you say we go up to the roof together and see how long I can hold him out over the edge?" He flashed a sick grin. "I'm in pretty good shape from the horses, but frankly this whole business has been damn exhausting. What do you think, ten minutes?"

"Mom!"

"Please don't," she pleaded and tried to grab for Christopher but couldn't catch him fast enough with her hands tied. "Please. Your men will be back with the money soon. Please let us go. Nobody has to get hurt. This is just about money. It's not worth it, Jake. You'll have what you want."

"Damn right I'll have what I want. And I'll have some fun in the meantime." He untied Christopher's foot and dragged the boy behind him.

Taylor had no choice but to follow. She thanked God he hadn't tied her legs. She stumbled on the stairs, made Jake wait for her. Playing for time was the name of her game. She needed to give Akeem enough time to somehow get away from the two thugs who had carried him off and get back here.

And if he didn't?

She hardly dared to think of that.

What if she was all alone in this, with an

armed man who was willing to do anything to get the ransom?

She blinked hard. Then she would find a way to deal with it on her own. Because, by God, she was not going to let anything happen to Christopher.

She moved as slowly as she could, scanning the staircase for anything she might be able to use for a weapon, but for the most part, the place was stripped bare.

The handle on the metal door to the roof looked promising, had she had a screwdriver to take it out and free hands to swing it at Jake's head. As it was, she had to pass by it with reluctance. She stumbled, took her time getting up, ignoring Jake's impatient swearing.

Christopher whimpered.

"It's okay, honey. Mommy is here."

However much she dragged her feet, they

reached the edge of the roof all too soon. Jake gave a demented grin in the starlit night, bending to grab Christopher by the ankles and upending him, dangling him upside down in front of him, swinging him like a pendulum.

"Mom!"

If she had nerves of steel, maybe she could have played the game longer, waited for Jake until he held her son over the abyss, kept him talking, given Akeem more time. But the desperate look in Christopher's eyes did her in and she lurched forward, toward him, falling to her knees to press her head to his small body.

"I'll tell you where the money is." She forced the words through her tightening throat, and apologized silently to Akeem. Because she knew that as soon as Jake had the money, he would be on the phone to his buddies to let them know that all further questioning of Akeem was unnecessary. And she had little doubt of what would happen after that. "I'll tell you everything," she told the man again.

"I thought so," Jake said and let Christopher fold to the ground.

Her son was immediately pressed against her, his skinny little arms wrapped tight around her neck.

"So where is it then?" Jake was asking.

"I'll show you."

He backhanded her once again.

And this time, Christopher charged at him, catching him at the knees and making him stumble back a little. For a wild moment, Taylor hoped he might go tumbling back and over the edge of the roof, but that didn't happen.

"Don't hurt my mom!" Christopher charged again.

Taylor dived for him before he could be harmed, throwing her body between the two of them. "I'll show you, but I swear to God, if you lay a hand on my son—"

"Get up and get going." Jakc shoved them.

The climb down from the roof went slowly. She made sure to keep Christopher up front so they both had to wait for the boy to pick his step. She was in the middle to provide buffer, Jake behind her with his gun aimed at the middle of her back, making impatient noises, swearing and shoving them now and then.

They went all the way to the ground floor, and once again she kept her eyes open for some sort of a weapon. She saw a couple of pipe chunks, but could find no way to pick one up unnoticed with Jake watching every move she made.

He shoved them along to his pickup at the

covered loading dock. As he opened the door, he nodded toward the one Akeem and she had driven here.

"And what in hell happened to Pete? Would you mind telling me that?"

She thought furiously, trying to come up with an answer that wouldn't make Jake overly mad. Their lives depended on his goodwill. And she might have hesitated too long, because he turned from that car, shaking his head.

"Never mind. I don't the hell care."

She was pretty relieved to hear that.

"Could you please cut the rope? I would like to hold Christopher." She turned to him as he was about to lift them up into the cab.

I'd like to hold my son before we die, was what she was thinking, and maybe it had shown on her face and reached some deep-down smidgen of conscience, because after a moment, Jake untied the rope.

"Thank you." Hope rose. If she could appeal to that remnant of conscience…

But Jake's eyes had gone cold and hard again already. "Get in."

She did so, helping Christopher, holding him at last, which was the best feeling in the whole world just then.

But as soon as she was up, Jake took the rope and tied her feet together. "You try anything, I just as soon shoot you. Just so we understand each other." He walked to the driver's side.

She said nothing, just held Christopher, who snuggled against her, burying his little head in the crook of her neck. With a child's instincts, he knew they were in trouble and remained silent.

When they got to the first gate, Jake gave her the key to the padlock instead of getting out himself, keeping the gun pointed at her son. He didn't have to say anything.

She got out, hopped over to the gate with painstaking care not to fall on her face, opened the lock and hopped back in. When they reached the second gate, past the guard-house, he gave her another key.

"Make sure you lock the first gate up," he said.

She did that, opened the second gate, waited for the pickup to pull through, locked that padlock and hopped to the car, but didn't get in.

"Let him go," she said instead.

Jake just laughed. "Any more brilliant ideas? Full of jokes today, aren't we?"

"Do you really want the death of a kid on

your hands? Do you know what the jury is going to give you for that? Let him go."

"I'll let you go together when I have the money." His tone turned mocking. "You're just gonna walk on out of here."

She wasn't willing to bet her son's life on that. "Let him go now. I'll catch up with him. If you don't let him go, how can I believe that you're going to set us free once you have the money? And if I think you're going to kill us either way, do you think I'm really going to lead you to those millions?"

She hated to be discussing this in front of Christopher, but she had no other choice. Either she saved his life now, or neither of them were going to live long enough to worry about how traumatized he became from being kidnapped. When this was over, she was going to spend as much time and effort as was necessary to make him feel safe again.

"You have nothing to gain by killing him. He's a four-year-old child. He talks about you every night before bed, you know. How Jake did this and Jake did that. Do you know that he thinks you're the best horseman on the ranch? Do you know that when Flint asked him last week what he wanted to be when he grew up, he said, *'Jake?'*"

She was telling the truth. Christopher was in love with horses and quick to hero-worship any man who worked with them. "He thinks the world of you. How can you do this to him?"

But as carefully as she watched, nothing in the man's eyes softened. Which didn't mean that she was going to give up. Not while there was still breath in her body. Of that he could be sure.

"This one is going to haunt you, Jake. How are you going to enjoy all that money?"

"You leave that to me." He glared at her, then shrugged at last and mumbled something about coyotes, then jerked his head toward Hell's Porch as he looked at Christopher and nodded to the open passenger-side door. "Scram."

Christopher wouldn't move an inch, of course. He was just a little kid, out in the middle of nowhere in the dark, scared to death. Not that he didn't have every right to be. But now he had been given a chance. Getting him to move was up to her.

She lifted him from the cab. "See that?" She pointed the way she'd come with Akeem. "Flint is there, waiting. You have to walk to him. I'll be right behind you."

God bless his heart, he really looked, peered hard into the darkness.

"I don't see him, Mom."

"Maybe you have to walk a little. Go on. Be a good boy. Go to your uncle Flint." She gave him a hug she never wanted to end, and a kiss on both cheeks, taking in his sweet, smudged little face, knowing chances were good this was the last time she would see him. "I love you, honey." Then she pushed him forward a little.

Akeem would come. Akeem could track. Akeem would find him.

"Are you sure?" He searched the darkness.

"Of course I am," she said when she was anything but. "You are such a big boy. You're not afraid of the dark, are you?"

That had him taking the first step. He wanted to be a big boy so badly. Being surrounded by cowboys all day long had him itching to be wearing chaps and working the horses with them.

She held her breath as he took another step, and another.

Since he wasn't going the way the pickup's headlights were pointing, his small form was growing less and less visible as he went.

She had no other choice, she told herself. This was his best chance. But knowing that didn't make watching him go any easier.

"I still don't see Uncle Flint, Mom," he called back when he was just a blur through the darkness and her tears.

"Keep going, honey. He's there some-where. Just keep walking straight and I'll catch up with you as soon as I can."

She was sending him into so much danger. So many bad things could happen to a little kid out here at night. She didn't even dare think of the wildlife. But with the desert, there could be some element of luck involved, a chance. When it came to a bullet at close range, the chance of lucking out was zero.

And she trusted Akeem, believed that whatever it took, he would come for them. Believed it enough to send her son into the wilderness.

She blinked her eyes, wanting to see him just as long as she possibly could, but Jake stepped between them, drawing up the gun to her chest.

"Now that the touching part of the night is over, where is my damn money?"

"You'll have your damn money," she snapped, her heart breaking because as she looked over Jake's shoulder, she could no longer see Christopher. She had missed that last second, possibly her last chance to see that sweet little shape, to escort it a few steps farther with her gaze in all that darkness.

"Now," Jake growled the single word.

Her heart was shattering into jagged little pieces as she pointed at the guardhouse behind them, behind the gate she'd just locked.

"You couldn't say that when we were there?" Jake looked like he might backhand her again.

She couldn't have said it, in fact. Christopher needed time to get as far from here as possible before Jake put his hands on that money.

He was going for the padlock already. "You better be right about this. Come on."

But she couldn't make her feet move as she heard her son's faint voice call out, "Uncle Flint? I can't see you," in the distance.

Chapter Ten

Akeem bided his time until he could see the silhouette of the refinery chimney against the night sky in the distance. Then he slumped to his left as if he'd passed out or fallen asleep, went for the gun with his right hand, brought it around and smacked the butt of the weapon against the driver's temple with full force.

The vehicle veered to the left.

He was grabbing the steering wheel the next second, reaching over with his other hand to open the driver-side door, then kicking the unconscious man to the ground, all with the pickup barely slowing.

And he was on his way.

He slammed the gas pedal to the floor, watching closely, the ground illuminated by the headlights, careful to avoid bigger rocks and potholes. Flipping the pickup over on this uneven terrain at this high speed would have been only too easy. He didn't think of the dangers, or the hundred points of pain that was his body, he just did what he had to do in that moment, then the next and the next. He had one thought only now—to get back to Taylor and Christopher in time.

FINDING PETE'S BODY in the guardhouse did not improve Jake Kenner's mood. He made

Taylor pull the dead guy outside, so he would have more room looking around in there.

She took her time, groaning under the weight, which wasn't all pretend. Pete hadn't been the wiry cowboy type. He had at least thirty pounds on her. She'd never been more eager to be done with a task, but she dragged this one out to give Akeem time to get back before Jake decided that the game was over.

"Where is it?" he barked at her. "I don't see anything. If you lied—"

"In there. I didn't see exactly where Akeem put it, but in there, definitely." She kept glancing toward the desert, but could no longer see or hear Christopher no matter how hard she tried.

"Stay where I can see you." Jake tossed the chair out, and it crashed into the hard ground less than a yard from her, making her jump. Then came a rickety old desk that splintered into pieces on impact. He was ripping the place apart.

She moved back toward the desert, one step then another, small ones at that, the rope allowed little. Jake had left the gate open this time. Not that she thought she could run from him, not with her ankles bound, but she wanted to listen for Christopher—who she prayed was brave enough to keep going forward—and keep an ear out for Akeem, too, hoping to hear him returning.

"Don't set your heart on it." Jake grunted. He could see her from the open door, just as she could see him. He was prying up a floorboard. "Your boyfriend is already dead. Either way, whether he spilled where the money is or not. Those boys can be rough."

She tried to tune out those words, and moved back a little more to put some distance between herself and the dead kidnapper. Then she sat on the ground. If she could untie the rope that bound her feet, she might be able to make a run for it.

"Get up," he yelled at her when he stuck his head back out. "And come closer." He pulled back to his work again. He had to turn his back to her to do that, which apparently he didn't much like. "Better yet, keep talking."

So he would notice if she moved, she supposed.

She pushed up to standing. "Once you have the money, you better hightail it out of here. Your friends can show up at any time, and if they do, they'll want a cut. It'll be two against one."

She didn't want him hanging around,

looking for Christopher. She wanted him away from the area as fast as possible.

"You just worry about your own troubles," he called back.

And since he didn't look out, reassured by her voice that she was still where he'd last seen her, she sat back down and went to work on the rope again. She might not have been a cowgirl, but she'd been around horses and tack most of her life; she'd seen a knot or two.

"Talk," he ordered when she stayed silent for a few seconds, focused on her task.

"It would work out better for you if you let me go, too," she said.

"You don't say."

Another floorboard flew out, then Akeem's duffel bag. Jake stepped out after it and upended it on the ground, kicked the contents around in the moonlight and swore at the tent and sleeping bag. "I don't see any money." He fixed her with a murderous glare.

"Keep looking."

"I thought I told you to stand." He kicked an empty canteen her way and it bounced off her shin.

"I've been walking almost nonstop for days. My feet are killing me." She offered an innocent excuse, but obeyed him. "You have nothing to gain by shooting me," she continued talking when he marched back in. "Everyone already knows you took Christopher. They figured that out as soon as you turned up missing the same day. Everyone knows that you're involved, but nobody knows about the others."

Silence in the shack.

"When this is over and I'm questioned, I'll

be giving their descriptions. The cops' attention will be divided. They'll be looking for the others while you get away."

"They'll be looking for me, too."

"Your buddies will be a priority. If they kill Akeem like you say they will, a couple of murderers…" She let her voice trail off. "And I'll be telling the police that you let Christopher and me go in the end."

Jake appeared in the door again, carrying Akeem's second supply bag.

"A couple of murderers will take priority over a kidnapper who already gave the kid back." He seemed to consider that.

"Right." Taylor held her breath. *Please, please, please don't think too much, just go with it.*

Jake upended the bag and rummaged through this one, too. "I still don't have the money," he said in a voice that had murder in it, crushing her hopes.

"It's in there, I swear. I saw Akeem carry the briefcases in."

Jake fixed her with a hard look, and hesitated for a moment. "If you're playing for time—" He kicked the empty bag viciously but then went back in.

She inched closer to the mess on the ground—all of Akeem's supplies—looking for anything she could use to cut her ropes or as a weapon. Food, flashlight, first-aid kit, extra blankets—not exactly a treasure trove of possibilities.

Then her gaze went to the dead guy who stared blankly into the night, his body twisted at an unnatural angle. She pressed her lips tight.

Akeem had taken his gun, but he still had Akeem's knife sticking out of his throat. She needed to overcome her revulsion and grab that somehow, because in seconds Jake would have the briefcases and would be deciding whether or not to let her live. She wasn't too optimistic about her prospects.

She shuffled toward the body, bent and reached for the knife's handle, froze when Jake whooped in the shack, held her breath and threw herself over the dead guy as Jake was coming out.

"What in hell are you doing to him?"

"I tripped." She flailed. "Yuck. Oh, God. Please get me up. Get me up!"

Jake laughed at her as he hurried by and put the briefcases in the pickup.

She had seconds only. She groaned with frustration when the knife wouldn't come easily. Her hand brushed against the man's front pocket. He had something in there. An empty pack of cigarettes and a lighter. She pocketed the latter. Maybe she could weaken her ropes with a flame if Jake got distracted by something long enough.

She moved back to the knife while pretending that she was trying to push herself up and away. Jake's boots crunched on the small rocks. He was coming back to her.

"All things considered, what you'd tell the cops and whatever, I think I prefer you dead." His voice was cold and hard. "One less witness if this ever comes to trial."

Her fingers wrapped around the knife's handle and it moved at last. But by the time she turned around, Jake already had the gun pointed at her head. He took in the knife with a surprised look.

"Too late, but it could have been a good move." He cocked the gun.

She lurched forward blindly, her feet still tied. This was the end. She had seconds. Akeem hadn't made it back. But she couldn't give up the fight, not even as she braced for death. She stabbed, kicked and screamed, but no longer saw Jake. She brought Christopher's sweet face up in her mind instead, wanted that to be the last thing she thought of before she died. Then the shot did go off finally, and she went down, hitting the ground like a sack of horse feed, gasping for air.

Jake's weight was crushing her lungs.

A second passed before she got her bearings and shoved him off, only to see Akeem running toward her in the moonlight.

She cut herself free from the ropes at last and stood as Akeem reached them, his gun still trained on Jake.

"Are you all right?" He rolled Jake over

with the tip of his boot, made sure he was truly dead before letting his gaze move to her, then drawing her into his arms.

She took only a second to scan him, to make sure he didn't have any major injuries. He walked and talked, she reassured herself. "Christopher is out there." She was pulling away already.

She reached for the flashlight that was among Akeem's scattered supplies on the ground, disappointment slicing into her when she realized Jake had broken it when he'd kicked it around.

"Let's go and find him. Which way?" Akeem was collecting Jake's gun and searching his pockets, his movements stiff. He might not have life-threatening injuries, but he was beaten and bloody.

She glanced toward the first-aid kit, for a

moment torn between helping him and rushing out into the night yelling her son's name.

He caught her. "We don't have time for that." He was opening Jake's cell phone. "Flint," he told her as he dialed, then talked into the phone when the call was picked up. "We're at the old refinery. We need everything you've got, choppers, ground vehicles, whatever. Christopher is lost somewhere around here." He listened. "She's fine." He listened again. "Yeah, I know it's hard to find in the dark. I'll send a beacon. You won't be able to miss it."

With that, he hung up and reached for a blanket from his camping supplies, ripped a long strip off, walked it to the pickup, unscrewed the cap on the gas tank and shoved one end deep inside before going around and getting a fistful of papers from the glove compartment. Then he opened the hood and bent under it.

"What are you doing?" She moved closer and watched him pull wires.

"Trying to get a spark."

And she understood at last. "How about this?" She pulled the lighter from her pocket.

"You're brilliant." He kissed her hard on the mouth as he took it and went back. "Start running."

"One more thing." She moved to the cab and pulled the two briefcases from behind the front seat, then took off.

He waited until she was a good hundred yards away, lit the end of the strip of cloth then hurried after her. They had maybe two hundred feet between them and the pickup before it exploded and lit up the night sky.

The sound of a helicopter came from a

distance, filling her stomach with dread. No way Flint could have gotten here this fast. "Who is that?"

"Probably the boss, coming to pick up his money." Jake took the briefcases from her and doubled his speed. "Jake wasn't the brains behind the kidnapping."

They had no time for her to ask where and how he'd gotten the information, and for the moment it didn't much matter.

The chopper dipped lower, apparently having noticed them in the light of the flames. Then whoever was up there opened fire.

SHE RAN BLINDLY, too scared to think.

"We need to split up," Akeem shouted behind her.

She heard him, but couldn't make herself go in any other direction except the way she had sent Christopher. He must have understood, because after a moment, he veered off sharply to the right.

She glanced back in time to see him run toward a clump of low bushes and dive among them, bringing up one of the briefcases for protection. The chopper went after him. Her heart about stopped. What was he doing? He would have been better off staying a moving target.

But when he returned fire at the chopper, and after a few seconds the helicopter lifted higher then banked to the left and pulled away, she realized he was doing the exact right thing, as he had been doing since he had shown up at the farmhouse and offered his money and his life to help her.

That they were still alive was a miracle. But they didn't have Christopher. She kept going, knowing Akeem would catch up with her, and he did within minutes.

"Christopher?" she yelled into the night. "Christopher, honey?"

He moved off and gathered some dried branches from the bushes surrounding them, lit some shriveled leaves that still clung to the tips and used the makeshift torch to light their way. "He'll see this from farther away."

Provided that he was nearby. He was just a four-year-old out in the dark. He could have veered off course, gone in circles for all she knew. He'd gone off over half an hour ago. She would *not* think that he could have already been carried off by a coyote or a cougar, or bitten by a snake and lying crumpled under a bush somewhere.

"Christopher?" Akeem called out. His

voice was deeper, probably carried farther in the night.

She listened carefully for a response that didn't come.

They walked on, taking turns calling out, stopped every once in a while to listen, but heard nothing beyond the usual night noises of the desert. They met no wildlife, which gave her hope, although all their yelling was probably responsible for that. They had likely scared every living thing away.

They moved pretty fast, rapidly approaching the limit of how far a little boy could have gotten in the given time. Her hope was dwindling with each stretch of dirt they covered now, fear gripping her heart tighter and tighter.

"Christopher?" She was hoarse. They both were.

"Mom?" A pipsqueak of a voice came from above.

"Christopher." She searched the branches above frantically. They were in a sparse grove of trees. "Christopher?" And then she saw a bulk on one of the branches.

It moved.

"I'm too scared to come down, Mom."

"Don't worry about that. I'll catch you." Akeem tossed his latest torch—he'd had to make a few as they'd kept burning down—and stood right under the spot, holding his arms out. "Just jump. I'll be right here."

Christopher hesitated. He didn't know Akeem all that well, Taylor realized. He'd been all alone in the dark, scared, traumatized from being kidnapped.

"We'll catch you together." She moved over and reached her arms up. "We are here now, honey. You don't have to worry about anything. You can trust Akeem. We can trust him."

"Are the bad men here?" He still hung on. "I'm scared of the bad men, Mom."

The fear in his voice squeezed her insides. "The bad men are gone. They can never hurt us again."

And then he shifted, and the next thing she knew, he was dropping into her arms, into Akeem's arms, which he held below hers to support them. She held Christopher as Akeem held the both of them. She soaked in the moment and let relief wash over her. The rush of emotions was making her knees go weak.

"I'm sorry, Mom. I couldn't find Uncle Flint." He snuggled into her, burrowing against her chest, his arms so tight around her neck that she couldn't breathe.

Which she didn't mind at all. She could

do without air. She couldn't do without Christopher.

"I've got you, honey. I've got you," she said, then couldn't stop saying it. "I'm here, baby. Everything is okay."

The sound of a chopper came, approaching rapidly. Her heart beat wildly, adrenaline rushing into her limbs all over again.

Then that first rush of fear hardened into resolve. She had her son back. Nobody was going to take him away from her this time.

"Get down." Akeem was covering them with his own body as soon as she squatted.

But he stood again after a few moments, and she recognized the sound of this chopper, too, the F28F Falcon Flint sometimes used to herd cattle. Next to Christopher's voice, it was the sweetest sound she'd heard in days.

"That would be your uncle Flint," Akeem

told Christopher and picked up his torch, grabbing her hand and leading them out into the open. "You are safe now. We are going home."

The chopper circled, then began lowering to the ground, the noise of the rotors too loud now to speak and be understood, so she couldn't thank him again.

But Akeem's eyes caught hers for a moment over Christopher's blond locks. And held.

Everything they'd gone through in the past three days was there in the air between them. Even the words they had left unspoken.

And she realized that maybe, just maybe, Akeem Abdul was better than all of her girlish fantasies. She had trusted her own life and her son's to him. Maybe she could trust him with her heart.

Chapter Eleven

"So you think it's all connected?" Flint asked after the police and Gary had taken off. Gary had stayed sober for his son's return. Maybe there was hope for the guy yet. Dr. Hardin, the ranch's very own physician, was gone now, too, having cleared Christopher and checked out Taylor and even Akeem, although he had resisted to the bitter end.

Taylor's pleading had done him in. There

wasn't much in this world he could deny those cornflower-blue eyes.

"There was this guy in a chopper before Flint got there. He shot at us at first, but when I returned fire, he took off," he told his friends.

"And?" asked Jack Champion, another member of the Aggie Four.

The three of them were together again, and like every time they gathered, Viktor's absence was a tangible presence in the room, something they all thought of but none would speak about. They were sitting in the living room at Diamondback, the house quiet around them.

"Just didn't seem like he was fighting all that hard for the money," Akeem explained. "Or that they had been in a rush to get the money in the first place. The front men, Jake and the rest of those lowlifes, yes. But I almost fccl likc the boss, whoever the bastard is, was playing for time."

"For what?" Flint asked. "What did time get him? He didn't get anything."

He gave that some thought, sitting in silence that was disturbed only by the faint whirring of the air conditioner. Suspicion built with each new thought. "If we're right and the boss was directing not just his men on the ground, but also had some influence with the police, he could have sent the cops to bust up that first exchange at the boulders."

"If he didn't want an early exchange, why did he agree in the first place?" Jack asked. "Would have been a hell of a lot simpler just to say no when you asked."

"He didn't agree. I negotiated that with his guy on the phone." Akeem rubbed his thumb over his eyebrow as he thought. "What did we miss out on in the past couple of days?"

"Other than the horse auction in Saudi you were so hell-bent on? How much potential profit did you lose on that?" Jack was somber, that famous smile of his that sent women swooning on a regular basis nowhere in evidence these days.

Akeem shrugged. His business mattered little when compared to Taylor and Christopher. But he would definitely look into that. He hadn't advertised that he would be bidding, but neither had he kept it a secret. It would be easy enough to find out who won the horses he'd had an interest in. "I'll do some research on that and let you know if something looks off there. What else?"

"I was supposed to go to Rasnovia." Jack grew even more thoughtful. "Our latest venture there hit a snag. Antitrust stuff. It's insane, just made-up charges that are coming out of nowhere. We're not that big. I was supposed to testify."

"Right." Akeem remembered now. He'd meant to talk to Flint about that when he'd driven out to the ranch then forgot about everything but helping Taylor when she'd run through that front door and into his arms.

Rasnovia.

Now that had some potential. There'd been a lot of trouble there lately. *Viktor.* His thoughts darkened. He hated to keep secrets from his best friends, but he could not do otherwise this once, not after having given his word.

Soon.

He told himself to be patient. It wouldn't take long before those secrets were revealed to all.

"I have to be back in Greece for an eight o'clock meeting in the morning. Then I have to make it over to Rasnovia to see what I can salvage from the antitrust hearing I missed." Jack was standing already. He clapped Akeem on the shoulder affectionately as he walked by. "Good to have you back in one piece."

"Thanks for rushing to the rescue," Akeem said.

Jack's choppers had been out there, too, combing the desert, going up in the air tonight against a police order. Having them around meant that they could divide the area up among them and Flint, which allowed Flint to find Taylor, Christopher and him that much sooner.

"Let us know what happens," Flint called after Jack, then leaned forward on the couch as the screen door banged closed behind their friend. "Do you think that's it? Rasnovia? We owe it to Viktor's memory to help that country. I'm not going to let anyone stop us from doing that."

"I think we need to check out the possibility." Akeem could think of a whole list of Rasnovian politicians and businessmen who might resent their interference in the country. There were a couple of budding capitalists who were keen on gaining financial advantage, and didn't much care about the means.

"Sounds like a place to start." Flint sounded bone tired after working twenty-four/seven to get around the police in the past two days, and get into Hell's Porch. He hadn't been able to get the chopper in the air until today, but he'd been out there in his truck, every day, searching. He *looked* bone tired.

And so was Akeem. "I should get going,

too." He glanced toward the stairs one last time before he stood.

Flint got to his feet as well, emotions filling those famously hard eyes all of a sudden as he drew a deep breath. "I never said thanks."

"You don't have to." He hesitated. "You mind if I check in on Taylor and Christopher?" He found it hard to leave without seeing them safe one last time.

Once they'd returned to the ranch in the chopper, the police and Dr. Hardin had separated them quickly enough, then Christopher had been packed off to bed and Taylor had gone up with him, stayed up with him. She probably wouldn't let her son out of her sight for a long time to come. He couldn't blame her.

"You should stay the night," Flint said. "Look at yourself. You're not fit to drive."

Which was bogus, and they both knew it.

Flint had seen him drive and do more than that in worse shape before. They'd gotten into a few scrapes during their college years.

"I should—"

"It's been a long time, Akeem. Don't wait so long again."

The air seemed stuck in his throat. Did Flint know he lusted after his little sister? And he didn't mind? "You think—"

"She's my sister. You're my best friend." Flint shook his head with a grin. "Guest bedroom is up the stairs, to the left." And walked away toward his wing of the house where Lora Leigh no doubt waited for him in bed.

He stopped before he would have turned the corner. "If you leave, do me a favor and set the alarm on your way out. Well, set the alarm either way, once you're done thinking.

But if you do go up those stairs—" he flashed a meaningful look "—I do expect there to be a wedding."

Akeem was too stunned to say anything back.

He stood on the spot for minutes after Flint was gone. He wanted Taylor, had always wanted her, wanted her forever. There had never been a doubt in his mind about that. In the past couple of days, he had realized that she was different now than she'd been before. And if possible, he loved her even more.

But would she have him?

Only one way to find out.

He walked outside to his pickup that one of Flint's men had found the day before and had fixed and driven back to the ranch. He retrieved something from the locked glove box, then something else on second thought, broke the prettiest rose off the bush by the door and strode back inside. He set the alarm that he'd never seen Flint use for as long as he'd owned the ranch. The events of the past couple of days had changed all of them, he supposed.

He sped his steps as he moved up the stairs, passing straight by the guest bedroom and going for Taylor's.

Her door was open. She sat cross-legged in an armchair, watching Christopher, who was sleeping spread-eagle in the middle of her bed in Spiderman pajamas, atop the quilt.

Her gaze lifted to him. "Are you okay? You should have gone to the hospital so they could have given you some serious drugs."

He took in the beautiful sight she presented, her blond hair freshly combed and falling over her shoulders, and emotions welled in his chest. "Not to worry. Dr.

Hardin gave me something that just about knocked me out. I think it was horse medicine." He was only joking. Flint kept the doctor on staff at the ranch for employees. Horse medicine was Lora Leigh's territory, actually.

Taylor grinned and stood, her wispy cotton nightgown falling just above her knees, moving gently around her body as she came to him.

His heart picked up rhythm.

"Are you staying the night?" She stopped when only a foot separated them.

Now that she was here, within arm's reach, a team of the finest Arabian horses couldn't have dragged him away. He handed her the rose. "Help me get settled in?"

She smiled and walked with him across the hall. "There are toothbrushes and whatnot in the bathroom cabinet."

He pulled her to him and wrapped his arms around her trim waist. "I'm going to ask for more than a spare toothbrush tonight, Taylor. I want you to know that I—"

She swayed toward him slightly. His brain shut down. He kissed her.

His head spun, and he didn't think it was from Dr. Hardin's potion. Taylor was soft, warm and willing in his arms. He'd waited nearly ten years for this, but it had been worth every second. And he was never going to let her go again. Which he would tell her as soon as they were done kissing. Which might take a while yet.

He took his time tasting her lips, no reason to rush now. For the night, she was his to savor, and he would make sure she stayed his for the rest of their lives.

He nibbled her bottom lip, then kissed the

corners, licked the seam of her mouth. And she opened on a sigh.

His hands explored her body while his tongue explored hers. There were no more reservations between them. The emotions swirling around them were too great to ignore or fight. And neither seemed to have the inclination to do that kind of battle.

He didn't break the kiss as he lifted her and carried her to the sprawling bed. He'd showered after they'd gotten back, and was wearing only a T-shirt and jeans on loan from Flint. Getting rid of them took no time at all.

When it was Taylor's turn, she helped him pull her nightgown over her head.

Enough moonlight came in the window to give him a visual he wouldn't soon forget. He dipped to kiss her as he covered her breast with a hand.

"Christopher?" he asked when they broke apart, remembering all of a sudden. He was treading new territory here.

"Sleeps like a log. Takes after Flint," she said.

And he grinned at that, remembering their frat days. He'd shared a room with Flint back in the day. She was right. A stampede wouldn't wake that man.

He got up and closed the door, locked it before he took off his underwear and walked to the bed, then stopped. "If he wakes up…"

"He never does." But she pointed to the baby monitor on the nightstand that she had brought over without him noticing it.

He'd been that lost in her eyes.

Worrying about a child was a strange feeling, but not strange bad. Christopher was a great little kid. Akeem looked forward to having him in his life. Fatherhood was no doubt going to bring some challenges, but he was looking forward to them. Looking forward to providing Christopher with some little brothers and sisters in time, too.

But not just yet. He should probably propose first. Except that Taylor was slipping out of her yellow lace underwear, and speech escaped him for the moment, his logical brain failing him on every level. He was lucky to be together enough to reach to the floor and pull a silver foil pack from his back pocket.

He touched her, tasted her and filled her. And experienced pure perfection for the first time in his life. Making love to Taylor McKade was sweet. And hot. Right. Crazy. The tight heat of her body seemed to have been made just for his.

He claimed her mouth, then her breasts, then her mouth again. And she gave as good as she got, making him wild with the small movements of her hips, the way she arched her back for him, the small sounds that escaped her throat when he reached deeper yet.

Their bodies soared together on the passion they wrought, twined together long after the last muscle spasm was spent.

Once his heart rate returned to within shouting distance of normal, he opened his eyes and touched her face, kissed her eyelids. Their bodies were still touching everywhere. "This is not just a quick thing." He kissed her lips. "I need to tell you how serious I am about us."

"Flint got to you, didn't he?" she asked with a dreamy smile as she pulled back to look into his face. "He can be a pest. It's the older-brother curse. I've tried to fight it. It's futile. What did he threaten you with?"

"Shotgun wedding at dawn," he said gravely.

Her eyes flew wide. "Wha—"

He grinned and kissed her again, covered her face with kisses. He took care not to leave out anything, not her eyelids, not her cheekbones, not the line of her chin. "Okay, maybe not at dawn. We could probably talk him into giving you time to at least pick a wedding dress."

"What a terrible thing to say! I'm going to need a lot more time than that. Why, the caterer alone…" She went silent. "Is this a—"

"Yes."

He slid off the bed and picked up his jeans, reached into the other back pocket. She rolled to her side to watch him, coming up on her elbows.

And her cornflower-blue eyes went wider yet when he went down on one knee, naked as a jaybird, with a diamond ring held on his outstretched palm.

"I'm hardly the always-professional businessman you might think I am. That's a media
image the company's PR people work on. I
lose my cool all the time. I lost my patience
that day when I gave Gary a ride home. I've
done things—You've seen some of the things
I've done. I swear I'm not the kind of man you
would ever have to be scared of."

"I know," she interjected.

"You do?"

"I'm grateful that you protected me in
Hell's Porch. Whatever you did to Gary
before that, let's just say I'm not that upset
over it. I feel safe with you. I feel my son is
safe with you. You saved both of our lives. I
love the warrior inside you just as much as I
love your gentle heart that worries about
being forced into violence."

Her full acceptance of him humbled him.

"Taylor McKade, will you marry me? I would like a chance to earn your trust." He waited, leaving his heart and hopes in her hands.

The air conditioner stopped temporarily, and they could hear the bugs in the trees outside, serenading them, frogs croaking the chorus. The moon bathed the room in soft light.

Taylor lay naked on the bed, still flushed with the heat of their lovemaking; eyes wide and glistening, the most beautiful sight there had ever been on this earth, he was sure. "You already have," she said.

She stayed as she was, frozen in time for a second, then lunged at him, knocking him over and sending them sprawling on the floor. "Yes!"

Then they were kissing and making love all

over again. He could never get enough of her. He couldn't imagine that ever changing as long as there was life in his limbs. Some time passed before he could go about finding the ring among their clothes and slipping it on her slim finger. Then felt reluctant to let go of her hand.

But she wanted to get a close-up look. "This is huge. Way too much," she protested, but she was grinning from ear to ear.

Seeing her happy and carefree in this moment was incredibly nice. He wanted to keep her like this forever, would do anything to make that happen.

"If you don't like this, then you're definitely going to hate when I drape you in desert ice," he said dryly, teasing.

"Desert ice?"

"My grandfather's diamonds. Have I ever

mentioned he was in the diamond trade back in the day? His father more so. My great-grandfather was a hired protector for the diamond caravans that took the gems from Africa to the Far East, traveling through Beharrain on the way. He tended to get paid in gems."

"A diamond collection?" She stared at him.

"If this is going to be a problem…" He shrugged. "I might as well tell you. The collection is fairly sizable."

"I thought you didn't claim your inheritance."

"I didn't. I gave up the land and the palaces. But when the executors of his estate looked me up, they had the diamonds with them. There was a giant blue diamond in the bunch that reminded me of the eyes of a certain woman. I couldn't let it go."

And, really, he was being modest when he used the word *giant*. The piece required a separate insurance policy and was kept at the supersonic safe at his company headquarters at the auction house. It would be his wedding present to her.

"So you kept them?"

"With a certain woman in mind." He wanted her in the sprawling bed of his penthouse, covered in nothing but diamonds. He had commissioned some stunning pieces of jewelry over the years, sometimes not even knowing why he was doing it. She had been married and the chances of her ever loving him had seemed hopeless.

But now that she agreed to spend the rest of their lives together, he would have plenty of time to make all his fantasies real.

"I love you," he said, and was gratified when she said, "I love you, right back."

"I can get used to the sound of that." He

kissed her. Might have gotten carried away a smidgen.

But she was all smiles when they broke apart for air.

"Is this part of your grandfather's collection?" She held up her hand a few minutes later as they lay in each other's arms. Moonlight glinted off the sparkling yellow diamond that graced her finger.

"No. I picked that locally. I want a Texas diamond for my Texas rose."

He wanted everything that was good in the world for her and her son. He wanted to spoil them rotten, not that he believed for a moment that she was actually going to let him.

Her beautiful eyes narrowed. "Between the police, the paramedics, Flint and Lucinda and this whole madness, when on earth did you have time to pick a diamond for me?"

"First day I ever saw you. Nine years, two months and eleven days ago," he said.

She stared at him in amazement and then broke into a smile. After that, they celebrated long into the night.

* * * * *